GIRL FROM MARS

GIRL
FROM
MARS

TAM

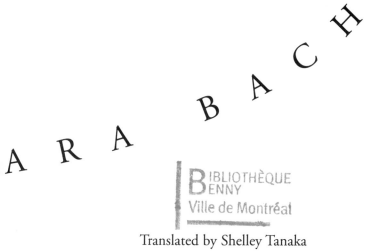

ARABACH

Translated by Shelley Tanaka

GROUNDWOOD BOOKS HOUSE OF ANANSI PRESS
TORONTO   BERKELEY

First published as *Marsmädchen* by Tamara Bach
Copyright © Verlag Friedrich Oetinger, Hamburg 2003
First published in Canada and the USA by Groundwood Books in 2008
English translation copyright © 2008 by Shelley Tanaka

Groundwood Books / House of Anansi Press
110 Spadina Avenue, Suite 801, Toronto, Ontario M5V 2K4
or c/o Publishers Group West
1700 Fourth Street, Berkeley, CA 94710

The translation of this work was supported by a grant from the Goethe-Institut that is funded by the Ministry of Foreign Affairs.

We acknowledge for their financial support of our publishing program the Canada Council for the Arts, the Government of Canada through the Book Publishing Industry Development Program (BPIDP), and the Ontario Arts Council.

ONTARIO ARTS COUNCIL
CONSEIL DES ARTS DE L'ONTARIO

Library and Archives Canada Cataloguing in Publication
Bach, Tamara
Girl from Mars / Tamara Bach ; translated by Shelley Tanaka.
Translation of: Marsmädchen.
ISBN-13: 978-0-88899-724-1 (bound).
ISBN-10: 0-88899-724-8 (bound).
ISBN-13: 978-0-88899-725-8 (pbk.)
ISBN-10: 0-88899-725-6 (pbk.)

Cover illustration by Hadley Hooper
Design by Michael Solomon
Printed and bound in Canada

"This small town hasn't got room for my big feelings"
— Björk, "Violently Happy"

Für Mams
und Julia, Anke und elis

PART I
Is anybody out there?

1

Name ———————————————
Address ———————————————
Date of birth ———————————————
Place of birth ———————————————
Height ———————————————
Weight ———————————————
Hobbies ———————————————
Favorite drink ———————————————
Favorite food ———————————————
Favorite film ———————————————
Favorite song ———————————————
Favorite actor ———————————————
Friends ———————————————
Likes ———————————————
Dislikes ———————————————
What I wish for you ———————————————

Name: My name is Miriam.
Age, date and place of birth: I am 15 years old. Fifteen.

Address: The town where I live is small and pretty. In the summer tourists come here to visit the church and the old fortress and wander through the streets of the old town. It's nice here in the summer. You can spend an evening sitting in a meadow overlooking the valley and admire the view over a bottle of wine. You can swim in the quarry during the day and sneak into the local pool at night. In summer you don't have to do much of anything at all. It's enough just to be here.

In the winter, though, this town is too small, and it's so cold the town itself freezes up. It's in the middle of nowhere, and suddenly everybody forgets about the church and the fortress and the old town. They even forget about themselves. They hide out instead.

I'm not a winter person.

I am Miriam. Fifteen. Blonde. Brown eyes. Average height, average weight. Daughter, sister, the person who sits beside you at school.

I'm Miriam, I'm tired, and that's it. No more, no less. Ordinary.

Likes and dislikes.

I dislike sports. My mother says I'm lazy. My math teacher says I'm not stupid. Sometimes I'm like this and sometimes I'm like that.

I stare at the book in front of me. We're all making these books about ourselves and passing them around to our friends to fill in the lists, maybe add pictures if they want. This fall they combined classes because our old class was too small, so now we're in a new class with new people. One of the new people passed her book to me and yesterday she got mad because I've had it for two solid weeks without giving it back, so I promised I'd give it back to her today.

You're supposed to describe yourself as accurately as possible.

Why does she want to know so much about me?

I leaf through the book. It's already half full. You can write whatever you want, but most people have just listed their favorite things, their likes and dislikes. Maybe stuck in a nice photo of themselves. Like this one of Bille. As if she actually looks like that. Fredi has covered the whole page with some kind of weird writing that's supposed to look like graffiti. Fredi, who has never held a can of spraypaint in his entire life.

Tap, tap, tap. Drumming my pen on the book. I have to give it back today.

What I wish for you.

I wish…

I wish I knew what to write.

Okay, imagine a girl. A stunning, talented girl that everyone admires. A girl people talk to and smile at. A girl who loves to smile herself.

Now imagine a girl that nobody likes, maybe because she smells funny or has a weird laugh.

I'm somewhere in between. Kind of pretty, according to my mother or the old guy who works at the newsstand. And kind of ugly, according to my brother Dennis and his friend Alex.

I am fairly smart according to my math and French marks. But if you look at my marks in history and chemistry, I'm the biggest idiot around.

So what are you, then, when you're always in the middle, not one thing or the other, neither fish nor fowl?

Boring, that's what.

So what should I write?

Friends.

Ines is sitting under the sink in the girls' washroom, copying out her math. Suse is sitting on the john smoking her third cigarette. She's talking about her new boyfriend. She only met him a couple of days ago, but now they're an item. His name is Martin, and she says he's really sweet and has a great body. He's eighteen and drives a Volkswagen Golf. A red one with a good stereo system — "He's picking me up in it later."

I imagine Martin. I can't see his face, because he's wearing a baseball cap and it's pulled right down over his forehead. He's wearing a beige or white sweater with writing on it, and pants of some kind. Behind him is his Volkswagen. Martin pulls Suse to him and she lets him. He kisses her.

Then he takes her hand and leads her to his car. She gets in. You can see the school reflected in the car windows. Then they drive away. You can hardly see Suse as the car drives off into the sunset. Maybe they're driving to the sea. Maybe to the mountains. Maybe he has his own apartment...

"What are you doing?" asks Ines.

So I show her the book.

"Ah," she says. Makes a face. "Whose is it?"

"Carola's."

"So, Carola does have friends," Suse laughs. "And apparently our Miriam fits right into the lovely Carola's yummy little inner circle." She sticks her finger down her throat and pretends to gag.

"So, you don't really like her?"

"No, not really," Ines says, and turns back to her math homework.

Friends. When our class was split, Ines and Suse went into the same class as me. I guess we belong together. We're friends. Or something like that. After all, we're sitting here together in the girls' washroom the way we do every morning.

Outside it's winter, and it's cold. Every morning is the same. Doesn't matter if it's Monday or Thursday. Five days of the week are exactly the same, because they are school days, and they don't make a difference. Every morning before class Suse and Ines and I sit here in the handicapped stall, the biggest one in the washroom. Suse always sits on the toilet and Ines sits under the sink, and we just sit here because it's cold and boring outside and so we smoke and wait…for something to happen.

7:23 a.m.: Can I copy your math homework?

7:30 a.m.: God, I'm tired.

7:35 a.m.: You little kids better move your butts!

7:45 a.m. (Bell rings): Just one more smoke — I'll be with you in a minute.

That's what it's like. That's what we call friendship.

Tap, tap, tap. Banging my pen on the book again.

Suse grabs the book out of my hand. She flips through it and laughs. Then she takes a drag of her cigarette and flips through some more.

"Yeah, right! In your dreams!" she laughs.

Ines looks up.

"What?"

"Kai writes here that he wishes he were a babe magnet. Can you believe it?"

"Give it back!"

Suse resists a bit, but she gives me the book.

I flip back to my page. The bell rings. Ines swears.

"One more smoke," Suse says.

I get up and look in the mirror over the sink, at me and Suse and Ines in the corner. I'm in the middle. I see myself standing there, looking in the mirror.

This is me. Blonde hair, brown eyes, average height, average weight. Every day the same.

It's winter and here I am, every day the same.

2

If a fairy godmother came and granted you three wishes, what would you wish for?

World peace. A cure for cancer and AIDS. A healthy planet.

No, now for real.

I'd wish for two thousand more wishes. Then for an alarm that tells me when I've reached wish number 1,999, so that I can wish for another two thousand wishes.

Actually, I'm perfectly happy the way things are.

Ha-ha.

But if I could wish for something that was just for me, and if I knew no one would judge me and say, "What?! You mean that was your wish?" then I would want...

There's this girl in the twelfth grade. I'd like to be just like her. She's tall and has wonderful eyes and hair and hands and stomach and breasts and...

I don't know. She's just beautiful. Not just because she was born that way. Look at her. The way she stands there.

For her it's just normal, but no one in this school — no, no one I've ever known — can stand as beautifully as that. And then maybe take a step to the front, just like that. And she moves her hands when she talks, and talks with her hands. It looks beautiful. And her voice is beautiful. Very deep. She speaks clearly and always knows what to say. She's in a band, too. I've seen her at a concert. And she has an unbelievable voice.

I'd like to be like that. Just like that. Beautiful. But not because I'm wearing the right outfit or makeup. Just because I am beautiful.

And I would also like to be really smart. Speak several languages and know more about politics. Like Florian. He knows everything about politics. But I don't think he just watches the news. He also reads five different newspapers and *Spiegel* and *Stern* and *Focus* and I don't know what else.

And I'd like to know more about history. Don't care about chemistry.

And then I'd like to have a talent. The girl in the twelfth grade can sing. Another kid in my class paints and draws wonderfully. Jane, who was in my class last year, plays the piano and takes ballet.

If I had all that, oh, man. If I could be someone like that, things would be really good.

But that is egotistical and shallow.

So, okay. World peace. An end to hunger and suffering and pollution.

"Miriam, your attention should be up here at the front!"

What? I was looking out the window, and the teacher doesn't like that. ("Your daughter, Miriam, daydreams too much, Mrs. Sander." "Oh, it's been that way since her first report card, you're not the first one to point it out." Ha-ha.)

If someone granted you three wishes, that means somebody out there wants you to be happy. Maybe a fairy godmother. A fairy godmother wouldn't scold me and say, "Now, Miriam, those are very nice wishes, but wouldn't it be better to think about the children in the Third World, who aren't as well off as you are, or about the melting polar ice caps? But if you would rather know how to play the piano, fine, so be it!"

"Miriam!"

"Yes?"

"For the last time, pay attention!"

"Okay."

"Stop staring out the window, or I'll close the blinds."

Now he's being silly.

"Okay."

Don't look outside. Look at the board. But I've already copied everything down.

Pay attention. But it's so boring.

We've been in this class for three months now. Most of the others already know each other, but I don't have anything to do with most of them. The other girls are scared of Suse and Ines. They're also a little different, the new girls. They wear sweaters with horses on them, and they go riding on the weekends.

Carola doesn't know that that's the worst thing she could say.

Suse: "So, Carola, what did you do last weekend?"

Carola: "I was with my horse."

Suse: "Oh, really?" Then she raises her eyebrows and gives her this huge grin, and Carola smiles back. But she hasn't known Suse since the fifth grade. She has no idea what she's really thinking.

Carola is sitting with a couple of other girls from her old class. Suse calls them the pony pussies.

In front of me, there's a row of boys who were in our class in the fifth grade, until they chose Latin. Now they're back with us, but they haven't changed one bit.

Someone in the front row is looking over at me. Laura. She's repeating the year, so she's new in this class, too. She sits in the first row where the keeners usually sit. She looks away and bends over her notebook.

She sits near Mario. I see how Mario signals to the other guys behind Laura's back, how he makes faces, how he shows off with that I'd-sure-like-to-get-her-into-bed look. Right. Mario is a real asshole. The other guys think he's cool. They call him Super Mario. He's the head of a bunch of idiots, which includes every single guy in our class.

What am I doing here, anyway?

That girl in twelfth grade? I have no idea what her name is. She probably has a spare right now and is sitting in the cafe around the corner. Or maybe she's in class and has just put up her hand and said something very clever about something that she saw recently on the news. Or about this article she read about women in Afghanistan. Maybe she's talking to her friends about important things. But like what?

Suse talks about her boyfriend. So does Ines. We talk about school and the other kids. About our parents. Sometimes we talk about music, a new CD we bought. I don't know. We just talk about stuff.

If I were only a little older. Fifteen is a funny age. Fifteen is so…nothing. So in the middle.

I look at my watch.

"Miriam, are things here too boring for you?"

He's really got it in for me today!

"No. Sorry."

"Just a few more minutes, okay?"

"Sure."

What time is it, again?

Ines is writing a letter to her boyfriend. His name is Florian. Flo. They've been together for almost five months now. They sleep together when they can, but Ines's parents don't like Flo. They don't actually have anything against him, but they don't like the fact that she's sleeping with him (having sex is what she calls it).

I picture Ines pushing the door closed behind her. I picture Flo undressing her. They have no music on, or else they won't be able to hear the front door open when her parents come home. I imagine her nosy little sister crying because Ines's bedroom door is closed and yelling, "What are you doing in there?" I imagine Ines's narrow single bed that probably creaks, so they do it on the floor or standing up against the wall.

I'd like to check my watch, but Schroeder's up at the front with his eye on me and I have to act as though I really am listening. When he looks away, I see that there's still seventeen minutes to go. God.

I look around the class. Carola and the others are writing. In the back row Felix is fiddling with something. Mario looks around at the idiots, points at Laura and makes a jerking-off gesture with his fist. So cool.

Laura is still draped over her notebook and looking up at Schroeder. Then she turns slightly to the side and writes something. I can tell from here that she's not writing anything. She's drawing or scribbling, but I can't see what it is. Schroeder should say something but he doesn't.

Then she looks up. Not really up. She just raises her glance and looks right at me, but she keeps drawing.

She has green eyes, like a witch. Weird. I can't look away and she just looks at me, just like that, just looking.

Maybe I should smile or something. Maybe.

Suddenly Schroeder is standing in front of me.

"Miriam."

"Mr. Schroeder?"

"Nice to see that you at least know my name. Now take this down. Homework for Thursday."

So I get out my daybook and write, Page 45, all of Number 5, Number 6 b to f, Read text 3.

3

When you live in a city, life must be different. Different from here. In this small town, every day is the same. I get up but I'm not awake. I eat but I don't know if I'm hungry. I drink but my mouth stays dry. It's winter but I'm still asleep.

Every day the same.

In a big city life must be different. I was in Berlin once visiting a pen pal. We went all over on the underground and got off at different stops and everywhere we got off things looked different.

"Smell," I said to her. "The way it smells here." We were in the underground station, there was graffiti all over the walls.

"What are you talking about?" she asked.

"Smell it. The smell here."

"Smells like shit, I know," she said.

Another time she showed me pictures from her vacation at a riding stable. "Right in the country," she called it.

But in the underground it smelled like City, like

chewing gum and dust and neon. It was a smell you could really get hold of. A smell that hit you in the face and went straight up your nose.

Whereas here everything smells so, so…I don't know. Sometimes a bit like earth or like rain or shit. But if you don't think about it, it doesn't smell like anything at all.

It's the afternoon. Afternoons are all the same. Go home from school. Eat. Clear the table, wash the dishes. Go up to my room, turn on the radio. Sit at my desk and do homework. Go back downstairs. Make tea. Look out the window, where nothing's happening but keep looking anyway until the water boils and I pour the tea. Maybe someone will phone and I'll talk and listen a bit.

In the city it would be different. In the city you can simply sit on the underground and watch the people. City people don't sit at home hiding out in their little houses with chimneys on top. In the city you can get on the underground, get off, walk around, look at things. And everywhere it's a little bit different.

Would I be different there, too?

I imagine what I would be like if I lived in the city. I'd have an underground pass so I wouldn't have to use my bike. I'd have friends who lived in old houses with balconies. I wouldn't need a map. I'd be out and about all day, I'd see people and do things. Interesting things, other things. Things I've never done before.

Instead I sit in this small town at my desk and finish exercise number five. It is half past four. In a few hours or so I'll be going to bed.

Shit, I'm bored.

No one else is home. The house is completely quiet.

Sometimes it can be really quiet all around, but inside everything starts screaming very loud, and you just want to scream yourself, or kick something or spit or bounce off the walls or something.

Sometimes I feel so big inside that I don't seem to fit.

I put on some music and turn it right up. I dance a bit. Then I sit by the window and look outside. I lie on my bed. I turn down the music and then I turn it off.

I lie on my bed and listen. It's an old house and sometimes you can hear the wood creak. The tree in the garden stretches its branches toward my window, scratches on the glass. Maybe it's cold and it wants me to let it in, like a cat.

At some point I hear my mother open the front door.

"I'm home," she calls, without expecting an answer. Someone turns on the TV. Dad has late shift. Dennis is in the hall talking on the phone. His voice gets quieter. Then he goes downstairs.

Sometimes you just hear this steady hum, like a neon light or a fridge. It's never truly quiet, but nothing is really happening, either.

I start thinking about a city and then I think about nothing. Then I turn on my music again and turn it up loud. Damn loud.

* * *

In the evening our house is even quieter. I stand beside my mother at the sink and dry a pot.

My mum is only pretty now and then. She has a loud laugh and isn't exactly thin. Since she started going gray she's been coloring her hair red. I don't think we look alike but everyone says we do. Once when I was little, I heard some stranger say, "Look, you can see that they are obviously mother and daughter."

Mum takes the pot out of my hand and puts it in the cupboard. Then she grabs a cloth and wipes the counter. Humming away, swaying lightly to the tuneless music on the radio.

"How was school?"

"Good."

"Anything happening?"

"No."

"Did you call Aunt Helene and thank her for the card?"

Shit. "No."

"Go and call her right now, or she'll be annoyed again. It won't take long."

"I still have homework."

"Still?" Oh, look, she's wrinkling up her forehead the way she always does.

"Yes!" Are you deaf?

"It'll just take five minutes, Miriam."

I'll bet entire countries have collapsed in five minutes. I wipe up after her with the tea towel.

"Get moving, Miriam."

"Okay, okay."

"The number's in the book. Under D. For Danz."

Do I look that dumb? I go to the phone, look up the number and dial.

It's busy. Ha!

"It's busy!" I call out in the direction of the kitchen.

"Then try again later."

I go back to my room, shut the door, sit in my chair by the window and pull my knees up under my chin.

A little later there's a knock on my door. Without waiting for an answer, suddenly Mum's standing in my room.

"I thought you said you had homework."

No, I lied, because I didn't want to call my aunt to thank her for a stupid card from Tenerife and then listen to her go on for hours about how long it has been, blah, blah, and how much my dear cousin would like to see me, blah, blah.

"I do."

"Doesn't look like it."

"How come you just march in here like that?"

"I knocked," she says crisply.

"Yeah, right." I stand up and stare at her.

"I did so, I knocked."

"But I didn't say Come in!"

She smirks, folds her arms and gives me this look that makes me so damned furious.

I can feel the anger building up inside me slowly, bubbling up like hot milk. Grrr.

"So, you didn't say *Come in*. Hmmm. Right. How

about if we just take the door off, and then you can stop worrying about whether I knocked properly or not?"

Arrrrgh!

"Well?"

"But this is my room!" I say, knowing only too well that it's like shouting at a wall, that my cries will fall on deaf ears, just like the slaves condemned to a lifetime of drudgery. They had no rights, either.

"Yes, but *your* room is in *my* house, and *I* paid for this door."

You see what I mean? What's she doing up here, anyway? It's always like this. If I told Suse and Ines what Mum and I fight about, they wouldn't believe me. So I don't tell them.

"So take down the door, then. I don't care!" I know I'm being ridiculous, but she started it!

"Fine!" She pushes *her* door open and makes a move to take it off its hinges.

"Want some help with that?"

"No. I want you to go and call Helene!"

Yeah, right.

"Now!"

Okay, fine.

Downstairs I pick up the phone and press Redial. It rings a few times before someone picks up.

"Peter Danz."

"Hello, Peter, it's Miriam. Is Helene there?" IhateherIhateherIhateher.

"No, Miriam, I'm sorry. Helene just walked out the

door about ten minutes ago. Can I give her a message?"

Yes, you can tell her that I'm sick of that bloody word door and that my life is shit and I want to puke. That's what you can tell her.

"Yes, could you please tell her thank you so much for the card, and give her a big hug from me?" There. Did it.

"Will do. Tell me, Miriam, when are you going to come and visit us? Sandra would love it if you—"

"Yes, it would be great, but I'm so busy right now— with school and everything..." Blah, blah. I can't hear any sounds coming from upstairs.

"Things going well at school, Miriam?"

"Mmmm." (Means yes.)

"Good. But call again. And don't do anything to disgrace the family."

Ha, ha. Very funny.

And he laughs a little, too.

"Okay. Bye." Hang up. I hate her.

Mum still hasn't come down, so I stomp upstairs. She's still standing in my room.

"Do you have to stomp around like that?" she says.

"Now what?" The door is still on its hinges.

"Did you call her?"

"YES!!!" She gives me this suspicious look, as if I might be lying.

"Good. You could at least dust and tidy a little more often." She rubs her finger along the top of the bookcase. "It's disgusting in here, Miriam."

"Doesn't bother me." Unlike you. If only she would just leave me alone —

"It will when the mice and cockroaches start moving in."

I want to tell her to just piss off. But instead I lean lightly against the desk, fold my arms and give her a crooked grin.

"Fine, do what you want, then," she says. "After all, it's *your* room." Then she leaves and slams the door behind her.

I win.

4

When I open the washroom door at school the next morning, Laura is in there rolling a cigarette.

"Hi," she says without looking up.

"Hi."

"You're the one who sits in the back row, aren't you?" Laura rolls up the paper, licks the edge, smooths it down.

What does that mean, the one who sits in the back row?

She looks up.

"Yes," I say.

Laura is sitting right on the sink. I can't just stand in front of her, so I sit down beside the toilet.

"What's your name?" She sticks a cigarette between her lips and lights a match.

"Miriam."

"Miriam." She inhales deeply, and her throat makes this little crackling sound. "Pretty name."

The door opens and it's Suse.

"Hi," she says when she sees me. "Why are you sitting —" Then she sees Laura. "Oh, hi!" And she shakes

Laura's hand (she shakes her hand!?). "I'm Suse." She sits down on the toilet and I have to shift over a bit.

Suse pulls a pack of Marlboro Lights out of her bag and lights one. She crosses her legs and rests one arm on her knee with her other elbow on top. She looks perfect. Between drags she achieves the perfect distance between her cigarette and her mouth. Graceful yet relaxed. Perfect.

I've never smoked a roll-your-own.

"And how do you like our class so far?" Suse asks Laura, looking at her with interest. A coffee in her other hand would complete the picture.

Why is Suse asking her this? We're new in the class ourselves.

"It's okay. All classes are the same, aren't they?"

Suse nods. Ines comes in.

"Here's your coffee." She hands Suse a cup.

"Thanks."

With Ines in here now it's really crowded. I have to slide over even closer to Laura. It's funny.

Laura crushes her butt on the floor and pulls out her pouch of tobacco again.

"You roll your own?" asks Ines.

"Yes. It's better. There's a lot of shit in those filters."

"And you think they're healthy without them?"

Laura looks up. "No, but it's cheaper." She finishes rolling the cigarette and hands it to me.

"Thanks." Did I ask her for one? I don't know.

Laura rolls another for herself, then gives us both a light.

It tastes totally different. Like country and hay. Maybe like leather. Mmmmh.

"Which class were you in before?"

"B."

"Katharina was in there, too, right?"

"Oh, yeah. Katharina was there." Laura gives her a crooked grin.

I'm feeling a bit dizzy. I don't usually smoke in the mornings. I'm staring at my cigarette, listening to Suse asking questions, Ines interrupting. I don't look at them. I hear Laura's voice beside me — soft, deep, louder than the others, closer.

I focus on the cigarette between my fingers and let Laura's voice wrap around me like smoke. I let her words seep deep inside me.

What time is it?

Laura used to live in Cologne. Her father still lives there, but she came here three years ago with her mother. Her mother works at home, freelance, Laura says. She has a little sister. She doesn't have a boyfriend.

She has three small rings in her ear and she's wearing a silver bracelet that she fiddles with when she talks. Her dark red bag is lying on the floor in front of her. She has a necklace of tiny red beads around her neck. When she smokes, I can hear that crackling inside her throat.

And then the bell goes.

Suse: "I'm just going to smoke one more first."

Ines: "I'm going to the bathroom."

Laura and I walk to class together. Take a step, breathe

in, take two steps, breathe out. Am I going too fast? Say something. Silence. Breathe. Maybe say something anyway? And then what?

It's hard. The door's straight ahead and I can't do anything except keep going, keep breathing. And I can't look at her.

I wish I could say something clever. Thanks for the cigarette. No, too lame. I wish I could say something that doesn't sound too much like I'm only fifteen. Something that sounds like the big city — Cologne, Berlin, Hamburg, New York, Tokyo.

But I can't think of anything.

"Hey, Miriam." Laura grins at me. She has her hand on the classroom door. Suddenly she lifts her arms in the air and nudges me with her hip.

"Samba!"

What?!

Laura opens the door and goes to her desk. And she doesn't look at me any more.

5

I have to go out. I have to do something, right now. My room is too small. It's afternoon again, and it's always the same. Too much the same, too small. Not just my room but this whole house, this town. I can't breathe here any more.

I get on my bike and ride—away from our house, fast, down the streets, away, faster, right out to the country roads. I ride and the cold rips my skin off with its claws. I get a cramp in my side. That's good. I'm freezing my ass off. That's good, too, because I can feel it all. I'm not hibernating like the other marmots any more. My heart is beating faster as I pump my way up the hill.

At the chapel I get off my bike. Tomorrow I'm going to be really stiff, but I don't care.

I look down. There's our school, our house and everything, but that's not all, there's more. All around are fields and forest. And beyond them the world keeps going.

The town looks so small; I'm so far away.

I stay until I get too cold. Then I get on my bike and coast back down the hill.

I've never been the new kid. Everyone here knows me. We've always all played together, or not. Evelyn was my sandbox friend. Then we made friends with Katrin and when they didn't like me any more, I played with Christian and Maja. And then I didn't, but somehow that didn't matter. Everyone knows me; probably nothing I do would surprise them.

I imagine what it would be like if I were from Mars, and I accidentally landed on this planet in this small town in the middle of nowhere. What would it be like not to know these streets?

I'm pushing my bike now. The trees are bare and a pale winter sun is shining. The sky is shimmering with cold. I'm wearing gloves, a hat, a scarf, layer upon layer… and I'm freezing. The cold is biting my face. I can feel it in my nose, on my cheeks, on my chin. I'm freezing, my face is freezing.

It's the end of February. I walk along and look at everything around me. I look at the houses. At the old lady who sits by her window staring up at the sky every day. A cat running along the fence. A lost glove that someone has stuck on a fencepost.

There's my old kindergarten. When I was in a bad mood I would wait there for my brother, clinging to the iron gate, holding onto the bars and swinging the gate back and forth every time someone came to pick up their kid.

I keep walking. There's the spot where I fell when we were playing some war game. I was wearing a new pair of shoes that Grandma had bought me the day before — shoes with smooth soles. When we all had to run, I slipped and broke a tooth. And my nose was bleeding.

Sometimes people move here, and they are the new people. They know people we've never met, streets we've never played in.

Once I sent my penpal in Berlin a few pictures to show her what it looks like here.

When you're new, no one expects anything from you, no one expects you to be the same as you've always been. Because they don't know you and don't know what you're like. You are the new person, so they don't know that when you were eight you laughed so hard that strawberry milk came out your nose. They don't know that you didn't get along with a certain teacher and have hated chemistry ever since. Or the way you looked when you were twelve.

At some point I stopped writing to that penpal.

When I go home now no one will be there. I'll make something to eat and then eat it and…

Someone is standing at the corner waving at me. When I get closer, I see that it's Laura and some guy. They're standing in front of a gumball machine.

"Do you have any change?" she asks me.

I dig a few coins out of my bag.

Laura says a quick thank-you and immediately throws a coin into the machine. Then she turns the handle and out roll a couple of gumballs.

"Shit!" She grabs the balls and sticks them in my hand. Then she puts in more money.

"Laura," the guy says, "it's bloody cold out here!"

But Laura is staring at the little trap door like a hypnotized rabbit, as more gumballs roll out.

"Fucking shit! It's not happening! I want the bloody thing. And now!"

She throws in the rest of the money, but again only gumballs come out.

I'm standing there with a hand full of red, blue and green gumballs. Laura turns the handle again desperately, but nothing happens.

"Are you sure you don't have any more change?" she asks the guy.

He shakes his head. He's wearing a necklace just like hers, with little red beads.

"You neither?" she says, turning to me.

"No, sorry." I'm standing here like an idiot holding these bloody gumballs that probably don't even taste any good.

"Laura, I'm freezing!" he says.

Laura doesn't say anything.

"The machine will still be here tomorrow!"

Laura smacks her hand against the machine, takes another look behind the trap door, and suddenly sticks out her lower lip.

"Man, it isn't fair! I must have put five Euros in that thing!"

"Life isn't fair, Laura." The guy takes her hand and

pulls her away and they run off down the street, while I just stand there holding the gumballs and getting mad. I look around for a trash can, and then Laura turns around.

"Hey, where did you go?"

What does she mean, where did I go?

"Or do you have other plans?" she says. Then she comes up to me, takes one of the gumballs, sticks it in her mouth and bites into it. It cracks.

"Shit, it's frozen." But she keeps chewing. She grabs me by the hand holding the gumballs and pulls me toward the guy.

He takes a gumball, too, looks at me and says coolly, "And who are you?"

"Miriam."

Idiot. If only I wasn't standing here with my hand full of these cruddy gumballs that I can't just throw away any more because Laura came back.

Wait a minute. I can still leave. I can say that I do have plans and then just hand over the gumballs or toss them in the garbage.

"This is Phillip. Phil," says Laura, and she takes the gumballs out of my hand and puts them in her bag, except for one, which she sticks in my mouth. "Miriam is in my class." Laura takes his hand, sticks it in my free one and shakes them both.

I feel the cold, round candy on my tongue. It tastes red.

"In your class, how nice," says Phillip. He lets go of my hand and shoves his in his jacket pocket.

I bite down on the gumball.
Crack.
It's definitely red.

6

I push my bike, which is glued to my hands, and follow them like a zombie, watching their backs. I feel pretty stupid. The sidewalk is far too narrow for three people and a bicycle. I can't hear what they're saying, not that I care what they're talking about.

I would like to know, though, what Laura wanted so badly out of the gumball machine.

I didn't even look to see what else was in there.

The farther we walk, the angrier I get. I'm mad at myself for running after them like a bloody dog. I'm mad at Laura for not telling me what we're doing and why I have to go with them. And I'm mad at this Phillip guy, because he's acting like an arrogant pig. Thinks he's so cool.

Laura is wearing a parka that's way too long for her. Now and then she runs her fingers through her hair and scrunches it up. She has short black hair that sticks out all over. You want to grab hold of it and scrunch it up yourself, just to see what it feels like.

Now and then Laura looks back and winks at me. Are they making fun of me?

Maybe I should just stop. The gumball doesn't even taste good any more. It's stale and getting tough. Gumballs from the machines are always shit.

I imagine them just leaving me behind or...or...I don't know. What does she want from me, anyway?

"We're here," Laura says.

We're standing in front of a house on the other side of town. I don't come over this way very often. We're practically in the country. A lot of the houses are only half finished, owned by young families who have planted small trees in the gardens and are waiting for them to grow big. Swing sets. Lawns that still haven't sprouted.

Laura unlocks the door and Phillip goes past her into the house. I stand there with my bike, still looking like an idiot. Miriam, the one "in your class" who has just pushed her bike all the way across town. No, don't bother inviting Miriam into the house with —

"Stick your bike over there by the tree. That's where I usually chain mine up," Laura says, holding the door open.

Slowly I wheel my bike over to the tree and chain it up where it's safe, where you can't see it from the street, even though no one would steal a bike around here anyway.

When I turn around, Laura is still standing in the doorway.

"Come on in! It's cold!"

Every house has its own smell, but maybe I'm the only one who notices. Whenever I visit Ines or Suse, the strange smell puts me off a bit. It smells different. It smells like other food, other soap, carpet and drapes, like dogs or canaries, maybe.

Here it smells like wood and wax.

Laura takes my jacket, half pulling it off my back, and hangs it in a corner with the others. I hear music.

We go into the kitchen. Something's bubbling. It's the coffee machine. Laura pulls the rest of the gumballs out of her bag and puts them on the table. She opens a cupboard and pulls out three mugs.

The kitchen isn't very big. There's a table by the window — an old wooden table full of dents. Everything in here seems to be made of wood — the floor, the kitchen cabinets, the doors — all brown and waxed. Scattered around are little pots filled with herbs.

Phillip is sitting at the kitchen counter ignoring me. Laura smiles at me. She fetches sugar, and milk from the refrigerator. She pours the milk into a little pot and puts it on the stove.

"This is the first single from their new CD," Phillip says. "I can burn it for you."

"Is it worth it?" asks Laura, stirring the milk with a whisk.

"Of course. But you really have to listen to it. I'm going to their concert in June."

"I don't have the money," says Laura.

"Really? Come on, you've got to be able to manage thirty Euros. Man, they're coming right to our area, you've got to go."

"We'll see. There's lots of time until June," Laura says.

The milk is getting hot. Laura stirs faster and takes the pot off the stove. Phillip takes the coffee pot off the machine and hands it to Laura. She fills a cup, adds a splash of milk and hands the mug to Phillip. Then she pours coffee into the other two mugs and fills them with milk. I sit down at the table, feeling like wood myself, because I don't know how to move, whether I should, whether I should say something or not.

Laura sits down at the table across from me and pushes the mug and the sugar bowl toward me. She smiles, and then she looks right at me and says, "Holy shit, do you even like coffee?" Then she starts laughing and can't stop. And somehow it's nice. It means Phillip finally shuts up, I have a coffee sitting in front of me and enough sugar to cover the Alps. While Laura is laughing, I put five spoonfuls in my mug. Stir it. Pull the chair closer to the table.

And then I sit there and listen to Phillip ramble on. Laura listens and smiles at me every once in awhile and at some point she gets out some cookies.

It's a little coffee party. I just sit there and warm up again, my hands thaw out. Laura rolls herself a cigarette and one for me, too, and I get a bit tired, even though coffee is supposed to keep you awake. But it's so sweet, and what with the cookies, and the cigarettes that wrap me up in smoke, and another new song on the radio, it's just so comfortable. One of those moments that just fits, that just feels right. You've eaten and drunk, you're not cold or sick. Those are moments that feel like fluffy fat cats sitting on the windowsill with their eyes closed. Listening to U2.

Laura is asking me little questions that she nudges over just like the cookies. Whether I've seen a certain movie. Whether I've ever played tennis. Whether my grandparents are still alive. Funny questions, but I answer them — sometimes yes, sometimes no, not much more than that.

And then it happens. Just like it always does, and just like always, I notice it far too late.

I start to hum. I don't know why I do it. It just happens, when I'm listening, or thinking about something, or writing. It's kind of like people who unconsciously let their tongues hang out of their mouths, except without the drooling.

Phillip is going on about how stupid some book was that he read "…and I struggled through three hundred and twenty-five pages and at the end all I could think was, so that's it? That's the whole thing? Three hundred and twenty-five pages." Then he shakes his head and Laura grins into her coffee cup.

Phillip suddenly looks over at me like he's angry, and I think, what an idiot. Then I realize that I'm doing it again. I'm humming.

Shit. I stop immediately. Maybe Laura didn't notice.

But she looks at me and says, "Can you sing, too?"

"No."

"Really?"

"No." Have never sung. Don't sing. Can't sing.

"What can you do, then?"

"Pardon?"

"Well, everyone can do something, can't they?"

"Yeah?" I ask. Right. I can spell my own name. I can still recite the poem "Erlking."

"I can recite 'Erlking.'" Terrific. Now I have really made a bad impression.

"I used to know 'The Bell,'" Phillip says.

"That's a really long one, isn't it?" Laura asks.

"Maybe," he says. "I don't know it any more."

"You see?" Laura says. "You still know 'Erlking' off by heart. I don't."

"You don't want me to say it now, though, do you?" I can just see myself standing on the table reciting 'Erlking,' and tomorrow the whole school will hear about it and I'll be disgraced forever, and here I wanted to graduate, or at least try to.

"Only if you want to," says Phillip, grinning.

"Another time, maybe."

Maybe? Never!

* * *

And before I know it, it's nine o'clock.

"I have to go now."

And then I do. I ride home and wake up a bit, ask myself whether I've been sleeping, wonder what I was actually doing there in her kitchen for all those hours.

7

Mum is still up.

"Where were you?"

"Out."

"Where?"

"At a friend's house. Someone in my class."

"Do I know her?"

"No." (I hardly know her myself.)

"Have you been smoking?"

"No, but the others were."

"You're not starting up with that shit, are you?"

"No."

"So whose house were you at?"

"Laura's."

"Laura. Ah. Have you done your homework?"

"Yes."

"How was school?"

"Same as always."

"Nothing new?"

"No. How about you?"

"No."

"Okay, then. Good night." I go to my room, get undressed, wash, brush my teeth like a good girl. Turn out the light and fall asleep.

* * *

Today is another day. And tomorrow will be another one. And then there will be others. But then again I could step out the front door and a huge rain could come down and sweep everything away. Or a big asteroid could hit BOOM. It happened to the dinosaurs. Could happen again.

I stay in bed.

Then I get up and go to school. I'm just putting my bike in the rack as the first bell goes and Suse has one more smoke and Ines and Laura go to our classroom, and as they're going in the door I'm still fidgeting with my bike lock. I go to another washroom, make a face at myself in the mirror and arrive in the classroom at the same time as Suse.

Quickly, quickly. Don't look anyone in the eye. I'm in a very bad mood. I'm tired. Yes, I overslept. I just don't want to talk about it. So? The whole world can just leave me alone. I don't need you.

Maybe the asteroid or the flood will come today, and I'll be the only one who's ready for it. The only one who will smile when it happens, because I predicted it.

I'm cool and calm. And very bored.

I don't want to look at Laura.

What is it about her that makes me feel so odd? Why does everything run so fast inside my head when she's around, so fast that I can't even grasp my own thoughts?

That I'm feeling so stupid. That I'm thinking that the first thing she told the others this morning was the story about me and "Erlking." Or about me doing the humming thing.

I don't want to look at Laura. And then I do. She is draped over her book scribbling something. She looks back, her green eyes flashing. She smiles, turns back to her book.

Suse leans over to me.

"Hey, I called you yesterday. Where were you?"

Didn't Laura tell her?

"Went for a ride on my bike. When did you call?"

"Around six."

"I must have got home right after that."

I'm really being silly. Who cares whether I was at Laura's place yesterday? And the thing with "Erlking," too. Who cares?

Sometimes it's like I say something and at the same time I am standing next to this Miriam, thinking, it's bullshit. Everthing you say is one big pile of bullshit.

But I don't want to tell Suse that I was at Laura's. I don't want Suse to ask me what we did, or why I was there. I don't want her to imagine what Laura's place looks like, or what it was like sitting in her kitchen drinking coffee.

She'll point out that I don't even drink coffee. She'll

want to know why I'm suddenly a coffee drinker. And what we were doing. And I'll say we were just sitting around talking and she'll say about what? And I'll say this and that, and Suse will say what kind of this and that?

Instead she'll just think of me as plain old Miriam who rode around town on her bike a bit and then went home when it got dark. Because that fits better. Because she can imagine that.

Today is Friday and that means the weekend.

"What are you doing this weekend?" she asks.

What am I doing this weekend? I am fifteen now. At fifteen you can't do much of anything. I can maybe stay out until ten o'clock on my own, without a babysitter. I can't drink alcohol. I can't smoke. And I can't have sex.

So what do we do on the weekends?

Suse's going to be with her boyfriend. Ines is telling her parents she's going to a girlfriend's house, but she's also going to be with her boyfriend.

Sometimes there's a concert in the gym, and if we're lucky, we get to go, and if we're really lucky, it's even good. Maybe someone will have a party. In some bars like the Erdbeereis you can get them to serve you alcohol if you're fifteen. There are possibilities.

At least I don't live in one of the villages around here, because they're even smaller than this small town I live in. At least here there are ways to get out of town. There's a small train station, there are buses, I have my bike.

Sometimes I just hope something will happen. Something that will take my breath away. Something more than "Ina made out with Patrick," or "Simone slept with what's his name" or "Matthias was so out of it that he puked for three hours." That's what people around here usually mean when they talk about "something happening."

And I'm there, too, hanging around, wherever — in the bar, drinking illegally, at a party, or maybe even at a concert, on a good weekend. The others get drunk, I get drunk, we argue, make out, dance. I'm there, too. Someone's the first to puke, someone's the last. I'm not saying that I'm better or different. It's just that when we wake up the next day, when I wake up, everything's the same and nothing has happened — nothing — even though they're all talking about it. Nothing has happened. Everything has just stayed the way it was. Everything's the same as always, except maybe I have a headache.

Every Friday I feel like I did the other day up at the chapel. I recognize, I feel and I know there is more to it than this. I believe in it and hope. It hurts a bit, but in a good way.

What are we doing this weekend?

Nothing. Nobody's doing anything. A few kids might know someone with a car. Then they can drive somewhere. To the beach, up to the mountains. Maybe someone has their own apartment. A couple will go to the movies and get a pizza. Or drink. Watch a video. A lot of kids will do nothing. Nothing at all. They'll sit around with Mum and Dad all weekend in front of the television.

Mum will bring out some snacks and Dad will get himself a beer and they'll all watch some movie or other. Then Mum and Dad will get tired and first one will go up to bed and then the other, and the last one left doesn't dare turn off the TV. Maybe you'll finish off the dregs of Dad's beer. Or maybe you'll sit in your room with the door locked and turn up the music and think how nice it would be to know someone with a car who could drive you to the beach or the mountains. You can go just about anywhere in a car.

And then you turn up the music just a tad, until Mum or Dad yells that it's too loud.

This town is so small it makes me wish I could grow long legs and run away, grow wings and fly. Something like that.

On Friday afternoon Suse has gone home sick, and Ines has to look after her little sister on the weekend, so see you around — maybe in the bar, or at the supermarket on Saturday when we're out shopping with Mummy.

What am I doing here? If I was a bird and had wings, I would fly away.

But I can't. I'm Miriam, I'm here, I'm fucked, I'm stuck. Loser.

So, what are we doing this weekend?

"What are you doing this weekend?" It's Laura standing at the door.

"Don't know." I'm walking toward the door, down the hall with the stone floor with snail shells embedded in it.

"What are Suse and Ines doing?"

"Suse is sick and Ines has to babysit." I say. I open the door to the schoolyard. Walk to the bike rack. "What about you?"

"Don't know," Laura says. As I bend over my bike, I glance up at her briefly. She's grabbing a fistful of her hair again. Her skin is pale. Her face gleams white in the daylight. "Phillip already has plans."

I fiddle with the lock. Phillip Shmillip.

"Hey." Laura leans toward me. "Do you want to do something?"

"Like what?"

"Go out?"

"Where?"

"Maybe to the Austerhaus?"

"That's in the city," I say, meaning the big city. The lock finally springs open. I wind it around my handlebars.

"So?"

"How will we get there?"

"I'll think of something."

I'm about to ride away, but Laura is walking beside my bike.

"Where were you earlier today?" she asks.

"Slept in." She's still walking beside me, even though her place is in the other direction.

"Ah."

I don't know how long she intends to keep walking with me, but if I say something now she might just turn off at the next corner.

"I'm sorry about Phillip yesterday," she says.

"What do you mean?"

"Phillip is really a nice guy. Honestly. It just takes him awhile to warm up to people."

Warm up. It's not like I wanted to kiss him goodbye or anything.

"He was the same way with me at first. Really."

We keep walking.

"Where does he go to school?"

"Kopernikus." A school in the city.

"And where did you meet him?"

"At a party." She looks at me suddenly. "We're not going together or anything. We're just friends."

I turn onto my street. Laura follows me.

Maybe I should just ask her where she's going. But that would sound rude. Maybe I should just…

"Hey, do you want to come in and have something to eat?"

We're at my gate. Laura turns to me, nods and grins. She holds the gate open for me.

"What are we having?"

I close the door. "I have no idea. We'll see what there is."

I hardly ever cook for other people. Never, actually. I just cook for myself. If Dennis is home, he cooks for himself, too, and takes it down to his room in the basement.

I look in the refrigerator. Hmmm. It's going to be tough.

"Is there anything you don't like?"

"Oh, I eat practically everything. Not crazy about offal. Or mushrooms. But that's about it."

Good. I cut up peppers and eggplant and zucchini, put water on to boil, open a can of tomatoes. Then I brown the vegetables.

"Do you like garlic?"

She nods. Good. Okay, garlic. The water's boiling.

"Rice or pasta?"

"Pasta." Right answer. What is she doing?

"Can I help?"

"No, it's okay. Do you want something to drink?"

"Can I have some water?"

Bottle, glass. And then we wait. The sauce simmers. The noodles are cooking. I stand there and stir them.

I hear the front door open.

It's my brother, Dennis. He doesn't say much. He's eighteen and he has his driver's license, but no car. Some of his friends do, though. He hangs out mostly with them.

And he lives in the basement. We don't have much in common. When I was little, he had to look after me a lot of the time, even though he wasn't that much older. Suse thinks he's cute, even though he doesn't have a car.

"Hi," he says. "Everything okay?"

I nod. Then he sees Laura.

"Hi."

"Hi."

Dennis stands there and looks at Laura, then at me. Then he goes to the fridge, takes out ham and cheese.

"Can I have some of those noodles?"

"Sure." I stir away like an idiot, while Dennis grates cheese and cuts up the ham. I drain the noodles and give him some.

"Is that enough?" Now go. Please.

"Yes. Thanks." Then he dumps everything in a pan and goes downstairs.

I put two plates on the table. Another glass for me. The noodles and the sauce. And then we eat.

Afterwards I wash up and Laura dries. And stays.

"Is it okay if I smoke?" I get the ashtray from the living room.

"So where is your room?" she says then.

"Upstairs."

We can hear Dennis's music humming from the basement beneath our feet.

8

It's funny seeing Laura in my room for the first time. The way she takes everything in — the books, the CDs and cassettes, my pictures and photos on the wall, the view from my window. The way she sits in my chair with a pillow in her arms and looks at me — looks at me in a way that makes me feel like a stranger in my own room, like it's really her room.

"Tell me about yourself," she says.

"Like what?"

"Anything." She pulls up her leg and hugs her knee.

"There's nothing to tell."

"Are you in love?"

What? What business is that of hers?

"No." I'm standing somewhere in the middle of my room and I don't know what to do. I look at Laura, then away, pull a few leaves off my fig tree. They're yellow. I should water it more often.

"So, have you ever been in love?" she asks.

There are a couple of leaves lying on the floor. I

pick them up and throw them in the wastebasket.

"Have you ever been in love?" she says again.

"I don't know."

"Why not?"

"Because I don't, that's why." So there. But I should be nicer, so I turn and smile at her.

"But you'd know if you were in love," she says.

"Okay, then, I haven't." I go to the bookshelf to get another CD. Laura is looking out the window. "What about you?" I ask.

"I think so, yes."

I reach for a CD. PJ Harvey, *Stories from the City, Stories from the Sea.*

"But you're not sure?"

"Who knows?" She grins.

PJ Harvey. Polly Jean. It's a nice name.

"Laura's a nice name," I say.

"Miriam's a nice name."

"Miriam is a boring name." I put in the CD.

"What do people call you, then?"

"Who?" My CD player always takes a while to find the song.

"Everyone."

"Miriam."

"Really? Not Miri?"

"Miri is dumb. What do people call you?"

"Laura. Lala. Mostly Laura." She looks at me again. "And you…"

"What about me?"

I press Stop, Play, but I can tell from the whirring sound that it's going to take awhile, that the machine isn't finding the song.

"You're a Mi, a Mimi."

"Mimi sounds like a senile old woman."

"And Mi?"

Mi? Sounds funny.

"I don't know. Like what?"

She thinks about it, then she says, "Hello, Mi. How was school, Mi? Look what Mi's done! Mi's looking pretty good today." She stands up, takes the CD case and looks at the photos in the insert. "So, how does that sound?"

I don't say anything.

"So, Mi, how does that sound?"

"It sounds… nice," I say.

"Anything can sound nice. How does it sound to *you*, Mi."

"Strange."

"Strange isn't bad," she says, as she starts singing along with the words.

9

When I look in the mirror, this is what I see.

Miriam. Brown eyes. Weird blonde hair. Not long, not short. Average weight. Not skinny, but not fat, either. And…I don't know. My face — nose, mouth, eyes, and ears, of course.

This is what I like about myself:

- my eyes are okay
- I don't have acne
- I have a small nose

What I don't like about myself:

- I have thin lips and a wide mouth
- no acne, but I do have a few pimples
- these bloody fingernails, the kind that keep splitting and breaking — it sucks
- fat stomach, fat thighs, flabby underarms
- ugly feet, but then, so are everybody's
- big ears that stick out
- then there's this big red blotch that I get on my left cheek; don't know why, it's stupid

- my teeth aren't very white

* * *

I've never been to the Austerhaus, the bar in the city. Suse and Ines have never been, either. Dennis goes sometimes, though.

It must be pretty good. Good music. No dress code, so I can just wear my sneakers and T-shirt and jeans.

Check the mirror again. I look like I'm dressed for school. Not for a Saturday night.

Okay, then. Tank top. Bangles. A little mousse in my hair. God, my hair looks like shit. Tuck it behind my ears? Okay.

Now what about my face? Black eyeliner. Try lipstick. Wipe it off again.

Sit in front of the television. Am I starting to sweat? Maybe? Deodorant. And maybe some…No, just deo.

On Saturdays there's nothing but crap on TV.

And now here comes Mum.

"Are you going out?"

I nod.

"Where?"

"Dancing."

"Who with?"

"Laura."

"How are you getting there?"

"With friends."

"Are they driving you home, too?"

I nod. We're watching MTV.

"Do you have to watch this shit all the time?" she says

"I just turned it on."

"Whenever I come in here, you're watching MTV. Do you have any idea how irritating it is?"

I say nothing. It's a new Madonna video. Madonna's always good.

"Always these videos. This one's already been on three times today."

"It's the first time I've seen it."

She's huffing behind me, but I don't look back.

"Besides, there's nothing else on right now," I say.

She sits down, takes the TV guide and starts flipping through it wildly. Grabs the remote, starts clicking channels.

Oh, goody. Rosamunde Pilcher. On a Saturday night.

"You're not serious, are you?" I say. Now she says nothing. "Hello?"

"If you don't like it, you can go up to your room."

I look at my watch and head upstairs as she settles back in her chair to watch.

* * *

Laura rings the bell. There's a car waiting in the street.

"They'll drive us," she says. I don't ask who they are or where she found the ride. "Ready to go?"

"Yes."

As we walk out to the car, she gives me a nudge. "You look good."

"Thanks." We get in. The music is so loud that I don't

have to talk. That's good. When we get to the city they let us out and keep driving.

The lineup is long. Behind me this girl is talking about how she's planning to run for student council. Another comes up to her and talks about the social injustice of the last electoral term. We inch our way forward. Some guy is talking about the ethics of feedlot agribusiness. And the price of a case of beer. Laura grins at me behind his back and gives me a drink out of her can.

Before we go in, we finish the beer and set the can down beside the wall. The bouncer looks at me, looks through my bag, waves me in.

"There, you see?" says Laura. "I told you. It's way too early for them to ask for ID." We walk through the rooms of the old warehouse with its high ceilings and metal scaffolding. Iron doors. Posters for concerts. Bistro tables.

"I have to pee," I say. I go to the white-tiled washroom. Have a pee, wash my hands. I see this face in the mirror.

On one side of me another girl is washing her hands. On the other side someone is doing her eye makeup. She gives me a short, blank look. I wonder what she's thinking.

I know what she's thinking. And I know what the other girl is thinking, too. I look at myself in the mirror and I know they can both tell how long I stood in front of my closet, how long I spent doing my makeup.

And through all of this, I can still see myself. I can still see me.

Laura's waiting outside the washroom. I stand beside her against the wall, sink down until I'm sitting on the floor.

"What's the matter?" she says.

"Nothing."

"Then smile!"

The eye-makeup girl comes out of the washroom and looks down at me. Her eyes are black.

"I don't belong here, Laura."

"Why not?" she asks.

"Because I don't fit in. Look around. I'm just fifteen…"

"But you don't look fifteen right now, you dummy."

"Yes, but that's what I am and I know it. It doesn't matter if the bouncer lets me in because he thinks I'm eighteen. I know I'm not."

"So why is that a problem? I'm not eighteen either."

"But you're different."

For a minute Laura looks as though she's going to say something. Then she slides down the wall to sit beside me.

"God, Miriam, nothing can ever be right with you, can it?"

"What do you mean?"

"There's always got to be something wrong. I mean, here you are, but you're not happy, the bouncer thinks you're eighteen, and you're mad because you're not. What is it you want, then, Miriam?"

"I don't know." I shrug and watch the people on the dance floor.

"Okay, tonight I'm going to be your fairy godmother," she says.

"You're drunk," I laugh.

But she grabs my wrist and looks into my eyes.

"No, really. Today I'm your fairy godmother. Today you can make a wish, and it will come true."

"Oh, yeah? Okay. I'll make a wish and you'll grant it." Laura nods.

"I want to have a good time tonight."

"And how will that happen?"

Laura is still holding tightly onto my wrist. It actually hurts a bit.

"I'll drink and dance, and the music will be good. And I'll kiss someone and fall in love a bit. And I won't throw up."

Laura looks at me with her big green eyes all serious, and doesn't say anything. Then she kisses me on the cheek.

"Your wish is my command." She doesn't let go of me. Laura is quite short, even a bit shorter than I am, but she pushes her way through the crowd like a bouncer and drags me to the bar. We find a couple of spots right at the bar and she waves the bartender over.

"This young lady needs something good to drink," Laura tells him.

"Oh, really? What will the young lady have, then?"

"Something good. Look at her and think what she would like," Laura says.

I stare at all the bottles behind the bar. It must be nice

to be a bartender and know how to make every drink.

The bartender looks at me. "Okay then." And a little later there's a sugar-rimmed glass with a straw sitting in front of me. I let Laura try it. Then we are jostled over to the dance floor. It's already pretty full. Laura takes a sip of my drink. It's sweet and sour at the same time, tastes more like lemonade than alcohol.

Then a song comes on that I really like — Jamiroquai. I start to hum along, but no one can hear me here. I move along to the music a bit.

Laura looks at me, takes the glass from my hand, sticks it somewhere and pulls me onto the dance floor. Somehow she manages to find a spot for me. At first I stand there like a bit of an idiot. Start dancing, for God's sake! But I'm not drunk enough yet. Laura smiles and dances for me. People are looking at us a bit funny, but it's nice how she's dancing there, with her arms in the air, swaying her hips back and forth, twirling around, snapping her fingers and smiling at me.

And suddenly I'm dancing, too, dancing for Laura and smiling at her, too — she holds me with her smile. Even if we do look a bit stupid. But the others don't know that Laura has just granted my wish. I'm dancing with Laura. I feel like I've never danced with anyone else before.

It's fun. We dance to one song, two songs, three, four — I don't know how many. Then we have a drink — Laura, too — and we dance some more and when our glasses are empty we go to the bar and get another. We stand there for awhile, laughing and maybe talking, even though it's way too loud to talk. We wink at each other, look at the other people and whisper into each other's ears.

"Who do you want to kiss?" Laura asks.

"I don't know."

"Look around."

There are a lot of people around. One guy looks over at us. Smiles.

"Him," I say.

Laura goes over to him. I'm embarrassed. What is she saying? But somehow it's thrilling to see her just walk over and whisper something in his ear. He looks over at me and smiles again. I try to read their lips, but I can't see their mouths.

And then he comes over. Laura stays where she is and just watches as he comes over and says hello. He sounds nice, even though I can't really hear him properly, but he puts his hand on my cheek, looks at me and smiles. And then he kisses me.

Just like that. He kisses me for a really long time, or maybe just for a second, and then at some point he steps back, takes his hand away and suddenly he's gone and Laura is standing beside me again.

"What did you say to him?" I ask.

"What do you mean?"

"Why did he kiss me?"

"Because you wished for it, Miriam." She takes a drink and pulls me back over to the dance floor. "I told you that today your wish would be granted."

And then she starts to dance again.

* * *

The last song isn't a slow one. "Girl from Mars." Laura knows the words. But I've had it. I'm leaning back against the wall. The wall is damp, and I can feel the plaster crumbling under my fingernails.

My pulse slows down. "…she never told me her name…I remember…a girl from Mars…"

The dance floor is empty. The song ends, the lights go on. I squeeze my eyes shut.

It's time to go.

Now I can see how dirty everything is here. How ugly it looks in the light. The high white walls, concrete floors and half-empty, dirty glasses, cigarette butts. Women hanging on to men's arms.

Time to go.

Laura and I go outside without saying anything. Laura's jacket is open. She has her hands deep in her pockets and she looks up the street. I'm glad she's not talking. She stands still and takes out her tobacco pouch. She sits on a bench and rolls a cigarette.

I look up at the sky. It's dark blue, riddled with stars. I hear the smoke rattle in Laura's throat.

At some point we meet up with the others. The radio is on as we drive back home. Late at night the music is quiet and right. Nobody talks.

Suddenly Laura leans her head on my shoulder. I take her hand and hold it tight.

10

Sundays.

"No, Ines isn't in. She left a few minutes ago to go to your place."

"Oh, well, I just wanted to ask her if she could bring along this one book. Well, thank you."

So Ines is with Flo —

Sundays are dumb. It has to be said again.

11

Have you ever been in love?

I'm fifteen. I've been kissed a few times. But I've never been in love. Or have I? I don't know.

* * *

The phone rings.

"Hi, it's Suse. What are you doing right now? I'm going stir-crazy, and Martin's busy. Are you free? We could ride around town a bit."

"I don't have time. I have to do this math thing and my mother wants me to help her clear out the cellar or something."

"Poor you! Okay. I'll try Ines, then."

"She's at Flo's."

"Whatever. I'll call you later or see you tomorrow, okay? Bye!"

I'm fifteen. I've kissed boys before. A few times. I thought I was really in love with Marco and then with Patrick that time during vacation. I thought I wanted to get married and have kids and that that was a real kiss I had with Marco the first time and with Patrick the second time. And I also thought I was sad when whoever it was didn't call me and things didn't turn out the way I thought they would.

* * *

The phone rings again. Dennis runs up the stairs, annoyed this time.

"It's for you!"

"Hi, it's Ines. Listen, I just wanted to tell you that I'm at Flo's but I told my mother I was going to your place."

"Okay."

"Good. What are you up to today?"

"Nothing."

"Well, have fun then."

* * *

But then I wasn't sad anymore. It's just kind of funny when I run into Marco or Patrick now. And sometimes I wonder why I kissed them. I like kissing. And when I've been drinking, then I really like it. Doesn't matter who I'm with. Maybe I feel something, too, but it has nothing to do with whoever I'm kissing. It's just the kiss itself.

* * *

"Mum, can I help with anything?"

"Why, are you bored?" Usually she always has some

stupid job or other for me. Why not today? "Something wrong, honey?"

"No. Nothing!"

I find the phone and call Suse. "I'm free now. I'll come over, okay?"

I grab my jacket and take off on my bike.

* * *

Suse lives on the other side of town. Her grandparents built this house for her parents. It has this big iron gate. That's the kind of a house it is. A house with a gate. A gate that's hard to unlock if you don't know how to do it. A gate that you might glue closed with Superglue on Halloween. That's the kind of house Suse lives in. And she lives on the top floor.

You can turn your music up here, and that's good. Suse likes to listen to music written by strong women who sing about men and women and love. Women who scream and wail but sometimes sing softly, too. Sometimes she copies out her favorite lines from the songs on her notebooks, on her pencil case, and on the wall above her bed.

The music is playing when I walk into her room. Suse is standing at the window smoking, but only because her parents aren't home. Otherwise she'd have to go for a walk to smoke.

Suse's room is big. There are scented candles everywhere, and cushions.

She flicks her cigarette out the window and closes it.

"So, your mother let you go out?" she asks and sits down.

Out? My mother?

"Um, yeah."

"Good, because I was so bored. You are a true friend, Miriam. Martin's playing football today and afterwards he's going out for a drink with the guys."

Football. Great.

"You don't want to go and cheer him on?"

"Go out to the back of beyond to stand around freezing my ass off? I don't think so." She pulls a bottle of nail polish out of a drawer, shakes it.

"Did you go out yesterday?"

She unscrews the bottle. "We were here at the club. I was totally drunk by the end, and then Martin's ex-girl-friend showed up and went berserk. Told me to get my filthy fingers off her boyfriend, like she's one to talk." She slowly paints her first nail, the one on her index finger. "Martin says his ex is the last of the great sluts, doesn't have a brain in her head and has no idea how to behave. She has to be home by eleven and after that has to go straight to beddy-bye — alone. But she thinks she's so cool."

She paints the second nail, quiet for a moment, then keeps talking. "No wonder Martin dumped her. I mean, how can you have a decent relationship if you have to live by all these baby rules?"

Suse looks up and I nod at her vaguely.

"Was she really bad to you?" I ask.

"Nope, Martin talked to her. Apparently she made a scene but she must be slowly getting the message that it's all over between them." Suse shakes her head. "It's pretty pathetic, actually. I feel kind of sorry for her. But I'm grateful to her, too, because otherwise I wouldn't have my sweetie!" With a few strokes she finishes her left hand, examines her paint job and waves her hand to dry her nails.

"I don't really know Martin," I say. I look around her room to see whether anything has changed.

"Martin is the best. And he's a great kisser! I can't imagine doing it any more with babies like Sven or Kai. They have no idea. Women mature earlier than men anyway, in general. We're two or three years ahead of them, right?"

The CD has come to an end. Suse looks up and says, "Can you stick in a new CD?" She waves her half-finished right hand at me.

I stand in front of Suse's CDs, which I've heard so often before. I even know which are her favorite songs on which CDs. And which songs remind her of what.

I test her. Anastacia. "I'm Outa Love."

"Oh, please, not that one. That's the song that was on when I kissed Kai for the first time." She groans.

"How was it, then?"

Suse looks up at the ceiling, as if she has to think hard to remember. Even though it was only six months ago.

"It was at a party at Anne's place. This song came on and I was so hot for him and we were dancing and then he kissed me."

"And how was it?" I ask again.

"It was just a kiss. When I look back it wasn't so great, but at the time I thought I was in love." Now she's painting her last fingernail. "But I wasn't."

"Are you in love now?"

Suse looks at me really seriously before she says yes.

"How do you know?"

"I just know. I feel it."

"And you didn't feel it with Kai?"

"No. Well, maybe, but not really, and anyway, I don't know, that's over and now I'm in love with Martin and there's no one else." She stares at me and blows on her nails.

I don't want to be here.

"Listen, I can't stay. I just wanted to see whether you were okay. That's the only reason my mother let me come over."

"What do you mean, whether I was okay?"

"You sounded weird on the phone. But, hey, you're good, so that's great. I have to go." I grab my jacket and bag and leave really quickly.

Outside it's clear and fresh and bright. It's a Sunday winter afternoon, and the sun will go down soon.

I pedal as fast as I can. There's not much going on. It's the weekend, the town's taking a time out.

Sometimes I think I'm the only one here. The only one who's not sleeping. The only one who's wide awake.

12

"What did you do on the weekend?" Suse says.

"We went to the Austerhaus," I say. I'm rolling a cigarette with Laura's tobacco.

"And what did you do?" asks Laura.

"I went out with Martin."

"Yeah? Where did you go?" I ask, even though I already know the answer. I concentrate on my cigarette, as if it holds the answer.

Rolling cigarettes is pretty difficult. Laura showed me how to do it.

"You went to the Austerhaus?" Ines asks.

"Yes," says Laura.

"How was it?"

Suse is quiet.

"Good. Wasn't it?" Laura gives me a nudge.

"Mmhhmmmh." Which can mean anything.

"What was the music like?"

"House? Trance?" Suse says suddenly.

"No, nothing so mainstream." Oops. Have to start

again. The hardest part is the actual rolling. After that you just have to lick it and smooth it closed, but the rolling is hard. If you want to do it properly.

"Hey," says Suse, "why don't you just take one of mine before you wear out your fingers?"

"It's okay." I'm getting it.

"How did you get in?"

"We just paid and went in."

"So they're not so strict about checking ID and stuff?" Ines can be very, very nosy at times.

"Nope."

"They couldn't be that strict if they let Miriam in," says Suse. Run your index finger slowly along the paper. Use your thumb to help.

"Maybe we can all go together some time," says Ines.

"Girls night out?" asks Laura.

"No, with Martin and Flo, too." Ines again.

"Martin just likes House and Trance."

It's rolled. Only the sticking down to do. Lick the paper, press it down. Finished.

Laura's looking over my shoulder. I can smell her skin and see her freckles. She smells like milk. It's weird. Like sweet milk. And a bit like wood.

She takes the cigarette, examines it.

"God, Mi, this one's perfect." Then she kisses me on the cheek.

Suse lights up a cigarette. And takes a deep drag.

13

History.

"Louis the fourteenth. Remember him? *L'état, c'est moi?*"

I couldn't care less. What is it about Laura? Every time I look at her, it's different. Sometimes it's as if she's always been here. (Of couse she's always been here. She has been in this class for a few months just like the rest of us.) And sometimes it's like she's here for the first time. For me. Like she's just landed on my planet.

And then again...

Then I look at her and she looks at me, and it's different again. Not bad different, but weird, like when you hear a new song that sounds strange but not in a bad way. And at some point you find yourself humming along, and you remember the words as you lie in bed, thinking of Laura and smiling into the dark, because the song is good, better than the others, and because it makes your heart beat faster, and it reminds you of yourself.

That's what it's like with Laura. It's weird.

My fingernails are all splitting. I pick at them, and bits of nail fall onto my history book. Outside the leaves are still falling. Behind the birches is my bike, and it's freezing.

I imagine what it would be like to just stand up, maybe grab my coat. Walk past the other desks, chairs, idiots who I've never exchanged so much as two words with. Walk past the teacher's desk, and it's all over now, baby blue. Stand up and use my legs. Look, outside there's a world that exists between 8 a.m. and noon. Outside there's life to taste and smell, and in winter it's cold. Then I just keep going. Leave this small town and go out through the fields and through one small village after another, even farther than I've gone on my bike. And maybe then I'll get on a train and keep going even farther. And maybe I'll get to some place that looks nice and I'll get off. And then maybe I'll stay there.

"Go on, read!" hisses Ines.

German. I'm reading out loud. Stumbling over the words. Then Ines reads. Then Patrick. And then the text is finished.

"What is the author talking about here?" Once again no one puts up their hand. Except maybe Gesine, who probably once swore to herself that she would always put up her hand and would always know the answer.

I can't even remember what we've just been reading. I look out the window again.

"I think…I don't know, but it sounds damned sad," I hear Laura say. I look up at the front.

"And why is that?" asks Lämmert.

"Because nothing's happening and he can't stand it," says Laura. "Because he's sleeping and he can't wake up, even though he wants to."

If I ever did stand up and leave, I'd take Laura with me, and later I'd ask her where she wanted to get off.

14

That evening I go up to my room. Turn on my music. Think for a bit, I don't know about what.

Outside something's moving on the balcony. I open the door and there's Dennis.

"Well?" he says.

Well? What does that mean? Does it mean how are you, or what are you up to, or God you scared me, sit down and tell me how your day's been?

"Well?" I say back.

Dennis leans against the balcony railing and looks out at the fields that start at the end of our garden. Then he looks at me, pulls a pack of cigarettes out of his pocket and holds it out to me.

I hesitate.

"You smoke, don't you?"

I look back into the house.

"It's okay. Mum and Dad are watching television."

So I take a cigarette and light it with the lighter that I keep behind the eavestrough.

Then we stand there smoking and looking out at the fields.

"What are you listening to in there?" Dennis asks, nodding in the direction of the balcony door.

"Do you want me to turn it off?"

"No. What is it?"

"It's a tape. Laura made it for me." She gave it to me this morning. A cassette that she made for me. For me. For Mi.

"Laura, eh?" he says, looking at me briefly. "Turn it up. You can hardly hear it." And then he goes back to looking at the fields.

I go inside, prop the door open with a flower pot and turn the music up a bit. Go back outside.

I finish smoking the cigarette and listen to the songs Laura put on the tape for me. Dennis has another smoke. And we don't say anything.

When he's finished, he crushes his butt and flicks it in the direction of the fields.

"Do you know what you need out here?" he asks as he turns around.

"No, what?"

"A bench. So you don't have to stand out here like an idiot. You need a bench."

And then he leaves.

15

Later the doorbell rings. When I open the door, Laura is standing there.

"Are you free?" she asks.

I nod. "What's the matter?"

"Things are shit. I want to do something. Can you come with me?"

I look back in the direction of the living room and call out, "I'm going out."

No answer, then Dad says absently, "Okay, bye." I take my jacket off the hook. We go out to the street and the door swings shut behind us.

"What do you want to do?" I say. "Get something to drink? A pizza?"

She shakes her head. "No. I don't want to see any people." She looks up. "Just you. Let's just go somewhere where we can sit and look around. I don't care where."

So I take her hand and pull her down the street as fast as I can. I pull Laura behind me until I start to gasp for breath, and she's panting and laughing. We keep running until the streets don't have any names any more, the town is behind us, there are hardly any houses, and then nothing more.

This is the highest spot around. A little hill in the middle of nowhere, with a bench. From here you can see the lights of town. The cars on the highway throw their lights like glowworms in the night.

We sit on the bench. Laura's breathing slows down. I can't see her face.

And then she says, "It's exactly the way I imagined it."

I'm still holding her hand and am a bit horrified when I realize it. I let go and look out at the houses in the distance.

Laura doesn't say anything else. She fishes around in her bag and then hands me a lighter.

"Can you give me a bit of light?"

I hold the lighter and the flame flickers a bit. Laura pulls her tobacco pouch out of her bag, stacks three papers together, rips a piece of cardboard from the package and rolls it to make a filter. Then she pulls a little bag out of her tobacco pouch and sprinkles grass over the tobacco on the papers.

I've seen all this before at parties — a small group huddled in a corner of the garden somewhere, sitting in a circle while one of them rolls and the others watch in silence, like they're witnessing the blood and body of Christ being turned into wine and bread. Maybe it's so funny because nobody talks, just like Laura right now. She's concentrating.

I start to say something, because it's too weird and quiet.

"This is one of my favorite spots. I got my first kiss here. Ever since then I've come up here by myself. It's probably a bit cold today, but it's really nice in the summer."

Laura holds the tip between two fingers, presses back the edges, examines her handiwork, clicks her tongue and says, "Pretty good."

I don't think she heard a word I said.

"I'm pretty proud of this, I have to say. Given that the light here is absolute shit." Then she takes my hand and puts it on her shoulder. "So, Mi, now you have to pat me on the back and congratulate me on this excellent rolling job."

I pat her shoulder a bit and pull my hand away. Sometimes it's so easy to touch someone and sometimes it's...

"Yes, congratulations. Great job," I mumble.

She seems satisfied. She burns down the tip, blows away the ash and lights the joint properly. She inhales deeply, waits and then lets the smoke out slowly. She takes another drag and hands the joint to me.

"You've smoked pot before, right?"

"Mmmhh." I almost believe it myself. I take a drag, get a lungful of smoke, practically have to cough. I hold the smoke inside me like Laura, my eyes fill with tears and I think I'm about to die when I slowly breathe out. I take another drag, this time more carefully, until my lungs are full, then I hand back the joint. Breathe out.

I feel warm. We are sitting on a bench in the middle of nowhere, somewhere in a forgotten galaxy. Time stands still. Maybe time is nothing but inhale, wait, exhale. Doesn't matter whose breath it is, yours or mine. The world only moves when you and I are breathing.

Below us the houses are lit up like Christmas. I'm not at all cold, even though it's winter. I take another drag, and my coat and my hat and scarf keep me warm.

Breathe out. My hands might be freezing, but I won't ask them, because then they can't complain. I listen to Laura's breathing, I can see the little glow in her hand, take it from her, breathe in, wait. The earth is spinning very slowly tonight. Breathe out. Everything is quiet. Peace on earth and good will toward men. It would be nice to hold her hand now, but I can't move, can't move my head. My gaze is fixed on the valley, on the lights of the little houses.

Suddenly Laura starts to talk.

"I had a really nice afternoon. With Phil."

The P-word.

"We listened to music and Mum cooked and we ate together. And then she told me she has to go away again, for three weeks or so. Three weeks. Maybe even longer. She just handed me some money and said she was pushing off, just like that. And I was pissed off. I told her that she should think about me, too, and she said I sounded just like my father. It was almost funny. No, actually it was sad. Phil just stood there and said absolutely nothing.

Nothing. You know? And then I got mad and threw him out. Shit." She sniffles. "Was it stupid of me to do that?" She looks at me, but I have no idea. Phillip. How do I know what he's like?

"Too bad he isn't here," she says, giggling a bit. "I think you'd like him when he's stoned. Although, what do I know? But I think you two could actually get along." She stops giggling. "In any case." Pause. Takes a drag. Talks again as she's exhaling. "Phillip is great. You can really have a great time with him. We're good friends. Too bad. Whatever." She's quiet again.

I smoke the end. The filter is getting hot. I throw away the butt.

Suddenly she leans her head on my shoulder, so all I can do is sit still and stare out over the valley.

"Go on," she says. "Tell me about your friends. About Ines and Suse."

But as I sit here, unable to tear my eyes away from the houses down there, I don't know whether they're my friends or not. I don't know what friends are, or whether I would talk about Suse and Ines the way Laura talks about Phil, even though she's mad at him. I don't know anything any more. I'd shrug my shoulders, but she's leaning her head on me and I don't want her to move it. I'm afraid that she'll take it away if I move.

"You're not saying anything." She giggles again, and I'm trying to think of what I can tell her.

There's so much I want to say and so much I want to know about her — so much — but my mouth is dry and my thoughts can't find their way out of my head. I feel so good so let's just leave everything like this. And leave Ines and Suse out of it. They'll spoil things.

"Mi, look at me." She flicks on her lighter and it lights up our faces. I turn my head toward her in slow motion. It lasts for hours.

When Laura sees me, she starts to giggle again.

"You're stoned! Ha! Look at you! Stoned!" Then she laughs out loud.

The corner of my mouth moves up toward my ears. I'm the Cheshire cat. I can't stop myself. My face muscles have a life of their own. I start to hum and try to remember which song it is.

"I'm hungry," Laura says suddenly. She takes my hand again, and my hand fits in hers like a little squirrel in its den. Slowly we walk down the path and this time she's leading me. I realize I'm singing this song and I have no idea where it came from. It was inside me, and now I'm singing, but where did I learn it? Doesn't matter, I just keep singing, louder and louder, all the way down the hill. All the way to the chip stand.

Hooray! And I'm thirsty!

"I'm thirsty, Laura!"

"Yeah, me, too!"

And then I sing some more and Laura squeezes my hand.

The streetsweeper is standing by the chip stand. We all know him because he says hello to everyone and is always so friendly.

"Two large fries, one with ketchup and mayonnaise and the other…?"

"With, um, mustard?" Yes, mustard. "And a Snickers bar. And a large diet cola."

The chip man is happy to make a little money at the end of the day, and I spend the rest of my money on the food, but I don't give a shit. I'm happy that I have a mouth I can open and stuff all this delicious food into. That I have teeth that chew and a nice chip man who really puts mustard on the fries. And that I have a throat so I can wash it all down with cola, and a stomach to hold it all. It's fun to eat. It's fun to watch Laura eating.

When we've finished, the chip man sticks two Jägermeisters in front of us.

"Here, girls, these will warm you up." And we say thank you politely, like good little girls. Laura starts giggling again, and the streetsweeper grins and takes a sip of his beer. I suddenly burst out laughing and start singing again. Then we take each other's hands again, just like little girls.

We keep walking, and then Laura suddenly stops and takes my face in her hands and presses her mouth against mine, very softly, very lightly. It lasts forever and for no time at all.

Then she pulls me into the Erdbeereis, where we see Mario and a few other kids, so we sit with them. Laura gets a pack of cards from the owner and we start playing a game of Mau-Mau. Mario gets us a beer. I win, Laura winks at me and plays badly, but she laughs.

This is probably the best evening of my life. Better than any evening I can remember. We have another beer and then we go back outside and Laura rolls us a couple of cigarettes.

I am only fifteen but it's great to be fifteen. I'm fifteen and I'm sitting in some street or other in the middle of winter and Laura is rolling us cigarettes by the light of a phone booth. And we are smoking and drinking and then I start to talk. I'm not singing any more. I'm saying ridiculous things like "In summer the sky is much bigger, did you know that? Bigger than in the city. Here the sky is gigantic. Much, much bigger. And in the summer you have to lie on the ground in the middle of a field, at night, of course, and then look up and when the sky is clear it's…the sky is so big and it's…"

Laura looks up and keeps walking.

"Like it is now?" she asks.

I look up and the sky starts to spin a bit.

"No. Not so wobbly," I say.

Laura starts to giggle again.

"I'm tired," she says. She stops. "I have to go this way."

"And I have to go that way," I say and point in the other direction.

We stand in the middle of the intersection, and I want to say, Laura, that was great. I want to tell her how much better and nicer and bigger it was than any evening I've ever had, but suddenly it's like before, and I can't get it out.

Laura grins and sways a bit, and I'm swaying, too. We are holding hands again, or still — I don't know. She pulls me toward her or I pull her toward me and her face is close. Then her mouth is on mine, this time longer and softer, and her lips are a bit rough. A little kiss, then another one, and my lips between hers become softer, warm. I open my mouth a bit and she opens hers, and I am kissing her upper lip, her bottom lip, and her tongue is stroking my lips, stroking my mouth.

I hold her hand. I want to be closer to her, I want to hold her face. Her lips are on my neck, her ears are cold, everything becomes warm and I am all flushed. My eyes are closed. And we kiss again and again, and...

Then I open my eyes. Laura looks at me — different, smiling. She gives me a little kiss.

And then she turns and goes.

How long do I stand here?

How cold it is all of a sudden.

PART II

It's life, but not as we know it

1

What are you really like?

1. Your crush flirts with someone else at a party that you have been looking forward to for ages. What do you do?

a) I go straight home and lock myself in my room with enough chocolate, tissues and sad CDs to last a week.

b) Who cares? I'll have way more fun with my girlfriends.

c) I make the best of things. I dance provocatively, until he can't even think about looking at anyone else.

d) I ask my best friend for advice.

What a load of crap. Next question.

2. On the bus, your friends standing behind you suddenly start laughing uproariously.

a) I turn around and start laughing, too, even though I don't know what it's all about.

b) I know for sure that they are laughing at me because I have once again done something super embarrassing. I want to dig a hole in the ground and disappear.

c) I tell them to shut up because I want to read in peace.

What?!

d) I report them to the bus driver.

Yeah, right.

3. Your friend asks to copy your math assignment.

a) I tell her that I don't understand the assignment myself, and she should ask someone else.

b) Sure, no problem. One of these days she'll do me a favor in return.

c) Never. What if we're caught? I'll fail, just because of her!

d) I take her aside and tell her that we can do the assignment together.

Oh, brother. What a pile of shit.

4. At the party that you have been looking forward to for ages, you see another girl wearing the identical top.

a) I run straight home and change.

b) I run straight home and stay there and never go out in public again.

c) I rip the shirt off the bloody cow and tell her that she'd better find something else to wear, maybe something that looks good on her for a change.

d) The girl and I laugh together about this hilarious coincidence and have a great time.

If such a thing were possible, then maybe there is a chance for intelligent life out there in space.

The clock says only five thirty-four. God.

Turn the page.

Or what about…

1. *A girl kisses you at the end of a wonderful evening.*

a) *Afterwards everything is great, and life is wonderful.*

b) *You think too much.*

c) *It was a mistake. It must have been a mistake.*

2. *If a girl kisses another girl, it means—*

a) *You're a lesbian.*

b) *You just haven't found the right guy yet.*

c) *You were drunk and stoned and not in your right mind.*

d) *What difference does it make who you kiss? Except for animals, that is. Ew.*

3. *If you spend your whole time trying to remember that moment, it means you are—*

a) *In love.*

b) *Forgetful.*

c) *Confused.*

d) *Even more confused.*

* * *

Five thirty-seven. The front door slams. I close the magazine, go downstairs.

Stomp, stomp, stomp. (Could you just once not stomp down the stairs?) I hear scraping sounds on the floor.

Dennis is trying to drag something through the door.

"What is that?" I ask.

"Don't ask dumb questions. It's a bench. Didn't I say

we needed one upstairs? Come on, grab the other end!"

And what if it was nice? Even if you can hardly remember it? What then?

"Where do you want it?"

"In the basement!"

Everything Dennis says has an exclamation mark.

"Over there! Watch out for my hand! Careful! Okay, put it down!"

If you have mainly checked a), then…

"We have to sand it down!"

"We?"

Dennis looks up at me with this expression he often wears — mouth open, cheeks red with effort, forehead creased.

"Yes, WE! You don't think I'm going to do this all by myself, do you? I've already dragged the bloody thing all the way over here!"

Okay, okay.

"Go and get the sandpaper!"

I do it.

Which answers would she check?

Which ones would I?

2

Favorite song.

"All I Want Is You" by U2. That is a great song. Bono does this thing with his voice that only he and David Bowie can do. It sends chills down my spine and makes me want to cry at the same time. He sings about this woman who promises him everything—gold, fame—but he says he doesn't want any of it. He only wants her. But then she breaks all her promises and it's so sad, because at the end he doesn't have anything, not even her.

That song is pain set to music.

Sometimes it's nice to feel sad. To go to the movies and sit in the third row all by yourself and cry. It only works in the afternoons and only when you go to see old films that other people have already seen.

Mum and I are driving into town. She wants to shop for curtains or some other shit at a special sale. She'll drop me off at the movie and pick me up later.

Some people think it's weird to go to the movies by yourself, but I like it. I also like going to the movies with other people, playing Guess the Ads, buying cheap candies at the bulk-food store and smuggling them into the theater.

The best films are the ones where there's no happy ending, though I like shoot-'em-up films, too. For some reason I love automatic weapons, even though I am normally a non-violent person. Must have something to do with the sound. So a film that ends with a graduation dance where the cheerleader and the captain of the football team get together is truly boring for me.

American Beauty. Everyone else has already seen it, and it's out on video. But I want to see it in the theater. Suse doesn't like going to movies, and Ines usually has even less money than I do.

The best seat at the movies is in the front half, even the first third, and right in the middle. One of my teachers once said the best spot to be in a movie theater and in a war is at the back, but he didn't know what he was talking about. Though maybe it is true for war, what do I know.

But my spot is taken. There's only one other person in the whole theater and he's already sitting there. Shit. It would be too weird to go into a practically empty theater and sit near the only other person in there.

I walk up the aisle anyway and look down the row. It's some guy eating popcorn, and he's looking at me, and he says, "Well, what a surprise."

It's Phillip.

I don't know whether to keep walking or turn around.

It would be even weirder to sit near Phillip in a practically empty theater.

He's still looking at me. Then he holds up his box and says, "Popcorn?"

So I sit beside him.

And he doesn't say anything, just sits there munching his popcorn and staring at the screen, which is empty. There's just this design of colors, moving to soft music.

"You really don't want any?" he asks again and holds out the box of popcorn.

I shake my head. I'm feeling bad already and now I'm sitting here beside this blinking idiot…

"*Phillip is really a nice guy…*" I can hear Laura's voice in my head.

If only I hadn't walked so far up to the front. If only I'd just sat a few rows back, then at worst we'd run into each other after the film was over and that would be it.

"Have you already seen it?" he asks.

"No." Of course not. Otherwise why would I be here?

"I have."

"Oh." Moron.

"Twice."

Sounds like someone with too much money.

"It's a good film."

Now he's going to spend the whole movie explaining what's going on, saying things like, "Keep your eye on the door, wait for it, now!" — just like the people who somehow always end up sitting right behind me.

"Besides, I was bored."

Then he shoves another handful of popcorn into his face and chews as he keeps staring at the screen.

* * *

Laura is totally normal in front of me. I ask myself whether it even all happened — the kiss, the kisses. I've been trying to remember it all week, but somehow I can't. Maybe because I had my eyes closed. That must be it.

But she is avoiding me. It's true that she is in the washroom every morning, but only when Ines or Suse are already there. We are never alone.

Maybe that's what she wants. I'll bet it is.

* * *

"Have you seen *Magnolia*?" Phillip asks me suddenly.

I nod.

"And? How did you like it?"

I cried my eyes out. "It was okay."

"Do you go to the movies often?"

"Sometimes."

"I do, mostly after school. I'm always killing time because the train schedules are so lousy."

How interesting.

* * *

She still smiles at me, but only when she's also smiling at the others. She's nice. Still offers me cigarettes. But she is so far away.

* * *

The lights go out and the ads start rolling.

"The Wild West!" says Phillip.

Oh, my God, he's guessing the ads. Someone please get me out of here.

"This one's easy. Marlboro. Their spots are always the same."

PLEASE!

"This one's for…a beer. No. But some kind of drink."

It is not! It's an anti-drug ad, you moron!

"Oh," he says when the logo appears — Don't Do Drugs.

"And that one's for…" Phillip pauses.

"Audi," I say.

"Do you think so?"

"No, I KNOW SO!"

He shuts up.

Then the trailers for the new films come on. He doesn't say anything about the first one. But then, "That looks like a piece of shit."

He's right, but I don't say anything.

"I'd like to see that one, but they'll never show it here."

"Why not?"

Because this is the asshole of the world and they only ever show Hollywood blockbusters here."

It's true, but Phillip looks at me angrily, as if it's all my fault.

* * *

Maybe I did something wrong.

* * *

It's a good movie. He was right. And he didn't talk once through the whole thing. And maybe I was just a bit snotty. I often am. And grumpy.

The ending is sad, and my eyes get damp — no, more than damp. I start to sniffle. Shit, not now. Not in front of Phillip.

He taps me lightly on the hand and hands me a tissue.

"Thanks," I sniff. He just nods.

We sit through all of the final credits. Then the lights go on and the doors are opened. We leave.

"What now?" Phillips says. He's staring at the notices for the other films.

"What?"

"What are you doing now? Do we want to get a coffee somewhere?"

"No, I have to meet my mother soon." He still doesn't look at me. "Do you want a lift back?"

He hesitates.

"No, forget it. I'm going stay in town for a bit. Take care."

And then he turns and leaves.

* * *

Maybe I did something wrong.

I definitely did something wrong.

Now all I have to do is make it right again.

3

Seven-nineteen. I've arrived at school too early.

"Laura, I have something for you."

"This is for you."

"Here."

"I made this for you."

I've made a tape for her.

"Laura, wait, I have to give you something."

"Hi, how are things? I made you a tape, too. Because you made one for me. And I thought…"

1. "All I Want Is You"

2. Jamiroquai, "Half the Man"

3. Lenny Kravitz, "I Belong to You"

4. "#1 Crush" by Garbage

5. "Sweet Jane" by the Cowboy Junkies

"Hello, Laura, do you have a minute? I have something for you."

* * *

The washroom door opens. Laura sticks her head in and looks around.

"Aren't the others here yet?"

I shake my head, look at her and wait to see what she'll do next. She stands in the doorway for a second, then pushes the door wide, comes in and sits down.

I have something for you.

Here. Just for you.

Listen to this.

She takes out her tobacco and starts to roll a cigarette.

"So, how are things?" she says.

"Mmmmh…" Plus head nod equals positive answer.

Here. Just take the damn tape!

"And how was the film?" she asks, still concentrating on the papers and tobacco.

"Which film?"

"Phillip said you went to the movies together."

"Phillip and I did not go to the movies together!" Shit. "We ran into each other there."

"So, was it good?"

"Yes."

In my pocket is the cassette with all the songs that I…

"I saw it, too. With Phillip." She rolls the cigarette. Looks at me. "Now we have something in common!" It's how she says it. She's smiling, but not really, not with her eyes. It looks as if she's really saying, "At last, finally!"

I won't give her the cassette.

It was a mistake.

I never should have kissed her.

But did I kiss her? Or did she kiss me?

SHITSHITSHITSHITSHITSHIT!

Laura lights her cigarette and then looks at me as she exhales.

No smile, no expression, no nothing. She just looks at me.

No, Laura, I have nothing for you. No cassette. Nothing. I'm sorry.

The door opens and Suse and Ines come in.

"Ta-da!" sings Suse. "Guess what? This weekend something is finally going to happen!"

I look up. What?

"Some of the tens and elevens are having a party in the old warehouse. Are you in?" Suse looks at me and Laura. I nod lightly in a way that could also mean maybe. Maybe.

Then I look down at Laura, who is drawing trails with ashes on the floor.

4

Ines and Suse are coming by around eight. It's three-thirty now. I'm sanding the bench with Dennis, and my right wrist is already aching.

"Aren't you coming to Miriam's?" Suse asked Laura at school.

"We'll see. I don't know yet. Probably not."

The old paint on the bench was thick, and on top of that there was a thick layer of gunk that I had to scrub away with cleanser. At least Dennis is helping with the sanding now.

"Can you sew?"

"What?"

"Well, you're a girl. Didn't Mum teach you how?"

"No, did she teach you?"

There's dust everywhere. I need something to drink. She is coming tonight, she said. Just not to my house. She must really hate me.

She kissed a girl.

"What are you doing tonight?" I ask Dennis.

"There's a party at the old warehouse."

"Oh, you, too?" This is just great.

"So, why can't you sew?" he says

"Because I can't! That's why!"

"I must have a serious word with Mum. With such poor womanly skills, we'll never marry you off!" Dennis grins through a small cloud of dust.

Ha, ha. Very funny.

But your sister kisses girls, so she'll probably never ever hook up with a man. Because girls who go for other girls turn into old lesbians. And no man will ever want her — unless he's allowed to watch.

Get it, Dennis?

Dennis takes another sheet of sandpaper and starts rubbing the next board.

"What color do you want to paint it?" I ask him.

"Not brown again." No. Nonono. It was so ugly. "What do you think?"

"I don't know." I have no idea, Dennis. All I know is that tonight will probably be the worst night of my entire life.

* * *

At eight o'clock Suse and Ines are in my room.

"Martin's coming around midnight to pick me up," Suse says, and I wonder whether Martin thinks that's when the coach turns into a pumpkin and the horses into mice. Ines is meeting Flo at the party, too. He's with his buddies.

My hair is still wet. I blow it dry and do my best to smarten myself up.

"Surprise!" says Ines, and she pulls a bottle out of her backpack. "Time to get warmed up!" Suse reaches for the bottle and opens it. It's some kind of sweet fruity sparkling stuff. Ines stole it from her mother's cellar. I've smuggled up a couple of bottles of Dad's beer. Suse drinks straight out of the bottle without ruining her lipstick.

We have lots of time. We don't need to leave until about ten. Suse has brought makeup with her and she's trying to get me to use some.

"Eyeliner?"

"No."

"Lipstick? Red?"

"No."

"But, Miriam, you'll never get a man this way." Ines takes the bottle and I get the feeling again that tonight is going to end badly. Maybe I should just stay home. No, I can't, not now that they're all here. I'll just go, drink a few beers and then say that I have a headache and leave. Yes. That's the plan.

"No, seriously now. What if a couple of nice-looking guys show up. Do something. We don't want you to be an old maid."

Ines snorts into the bottle.

Ha, ha.

I'm the old maid. That's who I am to Ines and Suse, though they don't really care that I don't have a boyfriend. They just want me to finally have sex. Don't ask! And don't even try to argue with them.

Flo was the first for Ines. Suse has already done it with eight guys, if I've counted correctly.

"Tonight could be the night," she says as she looks at my reflection in the mirror.

"You bet!" Ines squawks behind us.

"Tell me, is that your first bottle?" I ask her.

"Nope," she grins.

That's what I thought.

She holds out the bottle to me.

"Drink up!" says Suse.

And so I drink.

5

At nine-thirty, Dennis shows up.

"Hey, chickies. Want a lift?" He's hanging out with his friends in the basement.

"Sure!" Ines giggles and Suse touches up her lips with some gloss.

"Sure."

"I'm leaving soon. Be ready in about half an hour, okay?" The doorbell rings again.

"I'll get it," Dennis says, shutting the door behind him.

Suse falls back on the bed and laughs. "God, Miriam, he is so cute!"

I roll my eyes.

Someone comes up the stairs and Suse sits up when the door opens.

It's Laura.

And Phillip.

"Hello."

"Hi," everyone says.

And then I experience one of those moments when your ears suddenly plug up. They talk, but I barely hear them. Phillip sits near Ines and Suse and pulls out another bottle. They start to talk and keep drinking. Laura is standing there and I'm wondering whether I'm just imagining this whole scene.

"What do you want to do about getting over there, then, since there are five of us?" Suse asks.

"We'll walk," Ines says. Suse sulks a bit, then takes the bottle and drinks some more. Laura looks at me and suddenly starts to rummage around in her bag. She pulls out a CD.

"Can I put this on? I just got it today and I think it's really good."

Miriam nods. Miriam does not have a grip on things any more. Miriam's brain is no longer working well.

I see how Laura stands by the CD player and sticks in the CD, presses Play. I see that the others couldn't care less. The CD slides in and Laura pulls the CD booklet out of the case, opens it. She's reading the lyrics and moving to the music.

I am dying.

Dennis looks in. "Ready?"

"We're walking," Ines calls out.

Dennis nods. "Okay, see you later."

And I wonder how Ines is going to manage to walk.

* * *

In fact, Ines can't walk, and Suse isn't much better. Phillip has one hanging on each arm and he's struggling to keep his balance, though somehow he manages. Laura has the bottle and is walking behind the three of them. Me, too, but not beside her.

"Do you think anyone will be there?" I ask stupidly in Laura's direction. She shrugs, doesn't say anything, takes a drink and passes me the bottle. She's humming the song that she listened to three times earlier. Then she starts to sing the lyrics, only really softly. I can't even hear her properly. Something about "waiting here for you" and "wanting to tell you" and, I don't know, "for another day or two." She sings it over and over, like a mantra.

In front of us Ines starts to laugh and starts leaning to the left. The group staggers.

"A couple of people are coming tonight who I don't really want to see, you know?" Laura says suddenly, looking at me.

"Who are they?"

"From my old class. Just a few of them. Most of them don't matter. To me, anyways."

"And which ones do matter?" My stomach tightens a bit. I'm already a little drunk. Still thinking clearly, but a bit clouded by alcohol.

Laura looks at the ground and kicks a small stone into the ditch.

"It doesn't matter." She grins at me, but it's not a real grin. "Anyway, we're not going to let it spoil our fun, right, Mi?" She takes another drink. In front of us Phillip is trying to push Suse and Ines up the hill.

Laura doesn't say anything else. Then all of a sudden she runs up to the others to bum a cigarette.

And then we're here.

In one corner they've built a bar and there's a bartender selling beer, wine and strong mixed drinks called kamikazes. Dennis calls them Pussy Openers. The music is loud. There are a lot of people here. Suse stumbles into the crowd and says hello to a couple of friends. Ines looks for Flo, finds him and stays with him. I lose Laura. Phillip stays with me for a bit, but then yells in my ear that he's going to go and look for Laura.

This is one of those parties where you run into everyone you've ever known. Before long I see Laura on the dance floor with a beer in her hand. She takes a drink, looks at the people dancing and eventually disappears into the crowd.

I go and stand with Ines, Flo and Flo's friends. They're planning to start their own band, and they're talking about gear. Every now and then Ines kisses Flo.

I carry on. Suse sweeps past me and asks whether I've seen Martin.

"But I don't even know him."

"Really?"

"Besides, it's not midnight yet, so don't worry. He'll show up."

She thinks about it. "Do you have your cell phone with you?"

"Suse, I don't have a cell phone."

"Oh, okay. I'll ask Ines." And off she goes.

Whatever. I go to the bar and buy myself a beer, because Ines and the guys have finished off the drinks we brought. While the guy at the bar is getting my change, I spot Laura again talking with some girl I've seen before, and then she disappears again.

Maybe she's outside.

The air hits me in the face when I open the door and go out. There are only a few people out here. It's still too cold to party outside.

Party. I don't feel like partying. I think I'll go back to my headache plan.

I sit down on a bench and watch a car trying to park. The tires spin a bit, then the engine goes off, doors open and close. Maybe it's Martin.

Phillip suddenly sits down beside me.

"Hey."

"Hey."

"Everything okay?"

I shrug.

"Not you, too," he says, and starts to roll a cigarette.

"What do you mean, not me, too?"

"Don't tell me you don't know!"

Now I am really getting angry. I never wanted to come here in the first place. Suse and Ines wouldn't even notice whether I was here or not. Laura sure wouldn't.

"Laura's not having the best day, either." Phillip sticks the cigarette in his mouth. He lights it, leans his head back and exhales. "Still, it's a nice night, isn't it?" he says, looking up at the stars.

"So what the hell is the matter with Laura?" I shout at him.

Phillip sticks his free hand in his armpit.

"You know, it would be better if you asked her yourself." And then he says nothing more.

I stand up again and go looking for Laura. I shove my way through the crowd, see Suse kissing someone but I can't make out his face.

Laura isn't on the dance floor. She isn't at the bar or in the washroom. She isn't anywhere. Then I go back outside and as I open the door, she runs straight into my arms.

And I hold her, and look at her, and she looks at me.

And then she says, "I want to go home. Are you coming?"

6

Laura says nothing as we head down the hill. She's in a hurry. I practically trip a few times trying to keep up with her. She's smoking again, drinking another beer that she's brought with her. And she doesn't say a word.

I'm panting a little because I'm in such lousy shape. At one point I stop walking altogether.

"Stop! I can't go that fast." I sit down on a low stone wall. My head's spinning a bit. I should have eaten something, I realize. Breathe in, breathe out.

She looks at me briefly, takes a drag of her cigarette, tosses the butt on the ground and grinds it out.

"You okay?" she asks.

"I don't know. Are you?"

She shrugs and looks down the street.

"I'm cold. Let's go."

This time she walks more slowly.

* * *

On her street the windows are dark. Everyone's asleep. There's not even a light on at Laura's. She has to turn the key twice to unlock the front door. Inside she turns on all the lights and the music. She kicks off her shoes and flings them into a corner.

"Make yourself at home." She goes over to a cabinet and pulls out a bottle with brown liquid inside. I'm standing here in my parka with the big hood. It was cold outside, I realize. Pretty cold. My hands are red. I move my fingers and see them react to a message sent by some southwestern part of my brain.

A phrase suddenly occurs to me. *You led me on.* Why do I think of that now?

Laura comes closer. She takes my hand, presses a big glass into it and pulls me over to the sofa. The sofa is soft.

I remember the tape again. I put it away in my bedside table so I'd forget about it.

"I'm sorry," I say.

Laura looks at me and smiles suddenly. "Sorry for what?"

I shrug, but my big parka muffles the movement and turns it into a wooly sound.

"Hey, listen, drink up. It'll warm you up." Laura pulls her legs onto the couch and clinks my glass with hers. "Cheers!"

Maybe we're drinking too much.

I want to kiss you.

I shouldn't drink so much. I should have eaten something.

I'm sorry. I'm so sorry that it's making me completely sad.

Laura lifts her eyebrows in a question, but she doesn't stop smiling.

"Don't be mad, okay?" I say.

"But, Mi, I'm not mad!"

"But you were before. And yesterday. And I'm sorry, okay?"

Laura puts her glass on the coffee table. It makes a clinking sound.

Then she takes my hands, including the hand holding the glass, and says, "Dear, sweet Mi, I'm not angry or mad, and you haven't done anything to make me angry or mad. Okay?"

My brain sends a message to nod, and my head responds with slow up-and-down movements.

"So you're okay?" Laura asks.

Am I okay?

"How much have I had to drink?" I say.

"How much do you think you've had?" Laura asks.

"I don't know." I shrug my shoulders again. "I think my parka has swallowed me whole!"

* * *

No, I'm not going to be sick.

Really.

I'm tired.

"You're so cold."

She unwraps me. Scarf. Parka. Sweater. T-shirt. The

bathroom is very white and the light is too bright. I step out of my shoes. Laura stands by the shower and turns on the faucet.

"It's always too cold at first, so wait." She holds her hand under the water. My left foot steps out of my pants and pulls the right leg free. I'm not even wearing my socks any more.

Naked. Brrr. It's cold.

"That's good," says Laura, and she shoves me under the hot shower.

Better.

At some point Laura's hand reaches in the shower again and she hands me a toothbrush with toothpaste.

At some point I am very warm and very clean. At some point I am wearing a bathrobe and drying my hair. At some point I pull on a T-shirt that Laura hands me. At some point I pull up the covers and close my eyes.

The light goes out. The bed smells so good.

* * *

"Mi, are you sleeping already? I lied, Mi. I was in love once. With Katharina in my class. But she wasn't in love with me. And her boyfriend made my life hell. He was ready to beat me up. Are you asleep? Mi? You've fallen asleep. I was also in love with a guy. It doesn't matter who you fall in love with does it? No it doesn't. God."

Breathe in…two, three, four…breathe out…three, four…breathe in…

"I don't want to go through all that again. And I want

to be your friend, Mi. Okay? It's always good to have friends. So. I'm your friend. And I will not kiss you again, I promise."

Three, four...breathe out...

"Good night," she says very softly.

Breathe in, breathe out.

Tired.

Sleep.

7

Never again. Ow, my head. What have I done? When do I have to be home? How late is it?

I have to pee, but if I move, I'll wake up Laura for sure.

It's still early, barely light.

I get up very quietly, very carefully. In the bathroom I find my clothes and I get dressed. I fold the T-shirt and leave it on the side of the tub.

And then I go.

I'm a coward, right?

Yes. A real coward.

Sometimes I don't know what is really true and right. For example, I see strawberries and say, "They're red," and someone else sees them, too, and nods. But who knows if the red in my head looks the same as the red in theirs? No one can know that! Maybe their red looks the same as my yellow, or maybe it's just a bit darker than mine.

And I am a coward. On the way home I kick at stones.

I lose three in the gutter, one flies into someone's front yard, another under a car. So I give up.

A little fog wafts through the street. The sun couldn't get through even if it wanted to. It's not just the mist. There are definitely clouds, and behind them even more clouds.

Suddenly I smell bread baking, and I realize I'm hungry.

I still have money. Yesterday I only paid for one beer. Blech, beer.

* * *

At home I put the buns in a basket and put them on the table. I put water on to boil.

Look out the window. The neighbor's cat is stalking something. Two kids are playing soccer. A silver Beetle drives by. The water comes to a boil.

The first one up is always loud, no matter how much that person tries to be quiet. And today I'm the first one up. And I'm loud.

Soon Mum is standing behind me and kissing the top of my head.

"So, sweetie, awake already?" Then she looks at me and sniffs me. "Or did you just get home?"

I nod. Will she be mad?

"I slept at Laura's. I bought buns." Big smile. I'm a good girl!

It works.

"Okay, then," Mum says.

"Shall I pour you some coffee?" I ask.

"Oh, yes, please. You're an angel."

"I'm a good daughter!"

"Let's not go overboard."

We set the table together and I pour the coffee. Dad comes in, says good morning and then gets into the shower.

I eat a bun standing up and look out the window at the garden. The cat is now sitting on the lawn looking up at the sky. I look up, too, but all I see is sky. There's nothing there. No birds, no plane, no angels, no superheroes. Nothing to interest a cat.

I pull the curtains closed. I stand at the window for awhile thinking about Laura, and my stomach clenches until I feel like I'm going to explode.

After Dad is finished in the bathroom I go in myself, close the door, turn up the music and stand under the shower. My body becomes wet and warm, and I let the water run over my lips. My lips are so soft. I look down at how the water runs along my gleaming body. I wonder how all this can belong to me. I see how my knees bend, how my feet soften, how the water collects in my bellybutton. I hug my arms across my chest and close my eyes again.

How do you know when something is right?

I don't know.

I turn off the shower and dry myself, sit on the edge of the tub wrapped in my bath towel, until Dennis starts banging on the door and yelling that he needs to shower.

I go into my room and lie on my bed wrapped in the towel. And I stare and stare at the ceiling.

I don't need to get up ever again. Never. Ever. I will only get up again when I know what it is all about.

8

Outside it's bright out again. I lie on my back and look out the window, one hand stroking my stomach very softly, back and forth.

I dry slowly. The spot where my head was lying is damp.

I stand up in slow motion, put on a new CD, pull on my underwear and just stand there for a moment.

Someone knocks on the door and then opens it.

Why exactly do we bother even to have doors in this house?

"Are you coming?" asks Dennis.

"Where?"

"I want to go to the building supply store. Mum says I can take her car."

"Oh, yeah?"

"Yeah. I want to buy paint."

I stand there thinking it over.

"Hurry up, get dressed. You've got five minutes." Then he's gone.

* * *

Dennis has a funny way of driving a car. For example, when he drives backwards, he puts his right arm behind my headrest. Neither Mum nor Dad do this. And he drives fast. Oh, yeah, quite fast. He gets that from Mum. No, he drives even faster than she does.

"Where did you go last night?" Dennis asks as he skids around a corner.

"Away."

"So I noticed. But where? You couldn't have stayed that long."

I just shake my head and my neck muscles tense up as I watch the road. Dear God, let me make it out of this car in one piece.

"Do I need to worry about you?"

I stare at him in amazement.

"No!?!" Is he joking?

He pulls into a parking spot. Thank God!

As he walks across the parking lot he shakes the keys in his hand back and forth. Klingklangklingklang.

"Your friend Laura didn't stay that long, either," he says without looking at me.

I don't have to say anything.

He grabs a shopping cart and starts pushing it down the aisle.

"Did you two go home together?" he asks, practically shoving the cart into my calves.

"Hey, watch it," I snarl at him.

"Sorry."

I walk faster in the direction of the Paints and Finishes section. They've got paint to brush, paint to spray, paint for metal, plastic, wood. In white, blue, everything you can imagine. With gloss, with protective coating, metallic or antique finish and whatever. It's amazing.

"Well?" Dennis says again, keeping the cart at a safe distance.

"What about mauve? Or blue? No, I'm not crazy about blue."

Dennis grabs a can. "What about this?"

I look at it. "Dennis, that's forest green. You can't be serious!"

"Just a thought," he says.

I'm wavering between gold and mauve. Or maybe we should get…

"What's going on between the two of you, Miriam?" My eyes move from the label on the can to his face. "Between you and Laura."

"What should be going on? How much money do you have on you?" Gold is actually more expensive.

"Someone told me that Laura…"

"Told you what?"

Dennis takes a deep breath and the next sentence comes out in a rush. "Mischa told me that Laura hit on his girlfriend. He thinks Laura is…" He's looking for the right word. "Different."

Of course Laura is different. Laura is different from anyone I've ever known. Laura is different and that's good, because around here everything is all the same.

"Yeah, okay," I say. "Now I can tell you. Laura is from another planet. She's from Mars, and you know what? She's brainwashed me. And in exactly one month they plan to invade the earth. And I'm going to help them do it. That way I won't be eliminated."

Dennis stammers, "Miriam, I just meant…"

But I stick both cans of paint under his nose. "Gold? Good, gold it is. I'll see you at the cash."

9

I painted the bench by myself.

"No problem," I said to Dennis. It takes one hour before you can touch the paint but a day before it is really dry.

I clear away the newspapers under the legs of the bench and go up to my room.

Today time is standing still.

* * *

Not everything around here is bad. There are things I like. I know that when I'm older or grown up or both that I won't live here anymore. I might live in a big city, maybe even in Berlin, or…who knows.

In ten years I'll be twenty-five. What will I be like then? Maybe I'll have been in love with the same person for a few years. Maybe I'll have children, or a dog. I wonder what I'll be doing then. I picture an apartment overlooking a street full of traffic. At night drunk people wander down the sidewalk singing arias. Actually, I just picture myself standing there and looking out at the street below. Nothing more.

It's getting warmer out. I stand out on the balcony and smoke a cigarette butt that I've hidden. This is nice, the balcony. You can stand here and look out at the garden. Beyond that is nothing but countryside.

But what I really like about it isn't the fields or the trees, but the sky. The sky is so big here. In the city it always looks as though the sky has just been hung out to dry between the houses. But here it's different. At night the sky is a big black blanket with flecks of stars, a blanket that I can pull over my head when I'm sad. Or happy. A cool blanket when I have a fever. A warm blanket when I'm cold.

The balcony door opens and I quickly hide the cigarette butt with the others.

"Hey, sweetie?"

"Yeah?"

"How are you?"

"Okay."

Mum links her arm through mine. "Did you have a fight with Dennis?"

"Whatever." She hasn't noticed the cigarette.

"Love life problems?"

I shrug. Then we're quiet.

"There are supposed to be shooting stars tonight," Mum says suddenly.

"Yeah, I heard that."

"Nice, isn't it?"

And I nod.

"The sky is completely clear. We'll probably see some."

I've never seen a shooting star.

And then one falls. I see it out of the corner of my eye.

"So, did you make a wish?" Mum asks.

"No."

"So, think of one quickly then."

And then another one falls. What should I wish? I look over at Mum. I see her face looking up at the sky. And she smiles and in the moonlight she looks much softer.

Sometimes I wonder how everything can be so shitty most of the time and then suddenly completely different, so still and peaceful. Like the way she's standing here right now, her hair pinned up and with the moonlight shining on her face.

What do I wish for her? I wish her the best. I wish her luck and good health and then I wish that we wouldn't fight so much. So that she wouldn't have to be sad.

Another star falls.

"Did you make a wish on that one?" Mum asks.

I nod.

And Mum smiles.

10

"So have you ever had pets?" Laura asks me.

"A few. Nothing with fur, though. A few fish, a turtle that ran away. And a budgie."

"I had a budgie, too, once. But I killed it," says Phillip.

"What?" I say. Laura starts to laugh.

"Shut up, Laura!" Phillip snaps. "It was really tragic. He used to fly free in my room and one day I went into my room and forgot that I'd left the cage open. I slammed the door shut as soon as I noticed, but Hansi was caught in the middle."

Now Laura's really having a fit.

"What do you mean, in the middle?" I ask.

"I crushed him. With the door."

"Ouch!"

"Yeah, it was not a great moment," Phillip says, but even he can't stop smiling a little.

"It was my fault that our budgie Joker died," I say. "I left him out in the sun too long and his weak heart couldn't take it."

I still remember the Ferrero Rocher box that we buried him in. Funny. That box never showed up again.

"He was a good budgie," I say.

Laura raises her cup high. "To Joker. He was a good budgie."

"It's all a bit macabre, isn't it?" I say then. "I was pretty devastated at the time."

"Me, too," Phillip says.

"They're just animals," Laura says.

"Come on!" Phillip says.

"Why? If someone I really cared about died, that would be worse. A human being, I mean."

"I think the worst is for parents whose children die," I say.

"I would be the saddest if Pia died." Laura looks down at the table and starts sweeping a few spilled grains of sugar back and forth.

"Who's Pia?" I ask.

"My baby sister. She is so sweet. I miss her so much. She lives with my father."

Phillip stands up and gets himself some more coffee.

"Anyone else?" he asks, lifting the pot.

I shake my head, but Laura hands him her cup.

"When is your mother coming back?" he asks as he pours the coffee.

"Next weekend." Laura finally brushes the crumbs off the table. "Hey, listen, why don't we go somewhere next weekend—leave Saturday and come back on Sunday!"

Phillip shrugs and looks in my direction.

"Where would we go, and how would we get there?"
I ask. Just go somewhere? Can you do that?

"We just buy a ticket and go. Don't know where.
Wherever we want! Phillip, where should we go?"

Phillip thinks for a minute.

"I have an uncle in the east…"

Laura beams. "Isn't it great to have a big family? Here's
to family!" And she lifts her mug high.

* * *

"Mum?"

It's just before ten. The movie's about half over.

"Mmmmh?" Mum yawns.

"Mum, we're thinking of going away for the weekend."

"And who is we?"

"Laura, Phillip and I. We're going to go to Phillip's
uncle's place. Just for one night."

"And does his uncle know about this?"

"Yes." Does she believe me?

"And you'll be back home on Sunday?"

"Yes."

Mum yawns again. "Do you have enough money?"

"Yeah. It's really cheap if you go on a weekend."

"Okay then."

"Thanks!" Yippee! Wahoo!

Mum yawns again. "I can't stay awake any longer.
Turn the lights out before you go up, okay?" And she
goes up to her room.

I pull the phone onto the sofa and call Laura.

"It's okay. I can come."

"Fantastic. Phillip has already called his uncle, and it's okay with him, too."

The living-room door opens and Dennis comes in and sits down.

"I have to hang up," I say. "I'll see you tomorrow." Then I hang up the phone.

Dennis takes the TV guide off the table, leafs through it and looks up at the screen now and then.

The movie is extremely boring. I'll go to bed. I have a math exam in the morning.

"Hey, Miriam," he says. I stop at the door. "Everything okay?"

He turns around and looks at me. I can only see his eyes above the arm of the sofa.

I nod and then I go up to bed.

11

"So what are you doing this weekend?" Ines asks after math.

"We're going away for the weekend."

"Really? Where are you going?"

Laura didn't mention it this morning. I don't want Suse and Ines to know where we're going. And above all, I don't want them to know who "we" are.

"Heading east."

Ines nods and fishes around in her backpack.

"Are you free later today?" she asks.

I shrug. Look briefly at Laura, who is copying stuff into her notebook.

"Why?"

"I was going to drop by," Ines says and adds quickly, "I mean for real. I'm not just using you as an excuse."

"Okay. No problem." Laura closes her notebook and goes outside.

"When?"

"Around three?"

"Sure."

Ines hasn't been to my house very often lately. And I haven't been to her place in a long time, either.

I like Ines. I like her better than Suse. We've known each other since fifth grade, but always with Suse. When it was just two of us it would be me and Suse or Suse and Ines.

Ines has been with Flo for half a year. They met at some holiday camp last summer. Flo's okay, but sometimes I wonder how he sees her. She always looks pretty ordinary. I mean, when you look at Suse you can see that she thinks about what she puts on every morning. Ines just wears any old junk. Jeans and a sweater. Shoes. Jacket. Nothing special. Yet one morning when she came into the washroom she pulled up this plain gray sweatshirt and underneath it she was wearing a strapless corset. Dark red with black lace and bows and garters. And matching panties. All for Flo. She showed it to us like it was a new book or CD she'd just bought. As if it was totally normal.

Ines comes over in the afternoon. I get a bottle of sparkling water from the cellar, glasses from the kitchen and carry it all up to my room. Put on some music. Ines sits down and takes a glass but she doesn't drink anything. I really want to ask her whether she's here because Flo was busy, but I bite my tongue. That would be mean.

"So, what's new?" I ask her.

"Same as always. Oh, no, wait. Flo's actually allowed to come over on my birthday."

"Great. How come?"

"I'm turning sixteen."

Sixteen means not just alcohol and real ID, it means love.

Sixteen means that Ines can have her boyfriend up to her room with the door shut.

"What's new with you?" she asks.

"Nothing."

"Really?"

"Yeah."

"Something's going on with you, Miriam."

"What do you mean?"

"You're different. Is something going on that I don't know about?"

Who can I tell? Laura sure doesn't want to talk about it. And why should it be a secret? Why not tell Ines?

So I nod.

"Is it a secret?"

"Yes," I say.

"A good one or a bad one?" Ines frowns.

"Good. I think," I add quickly.

"Are you in love?"

I nod gently.

She grins. "So, who is it? Do I know him?"

And then I wonder if she will really understand. That there is no "him." That it's Laura. And I don't know any more whether I know Ines well enough, because I don't know how she will react.

"No."

"So? How long has it been going on? Are you sleeping together?"

"No."

Ines leans forward a bit and a bit of soda spills onto my carpet.

"Does he even know?"

I shake my head.

"Why not?"

"Because. It's complicated."

"But why?"

"Because he (he!)…just wants to be friends."

"Oh, shit." Ines finally takes a sip from her glass. "So what are you going to do now?"

"I don't know. Besides, everything's good the way it is. Maybe it's better this way. You can never have enough friends, right?"

Ines shrugs her shoulders and puts down her glass. She stands up and opens the balcony door, sits on the bench and lights a cigarette.

"Do you have the hots for him?"

"What do you mean?"

"You know, do you want to touch him and kiss him and everything."

"Yes."

"There, see? Having friends is all well and good. But love is also great. Maybe even a bit better." Ines grins at me.

"Yeah?"

"So what are you waiting for?"

I grin and shrug. Then I go out to the balcony and take a drag from her cigarette.

12

At eight o'clock Saturday morning I'm at the train station standing on platform three. Eight o'clock! There's just one old lady here sitting on a bench with her shopping bags. I'm carrying my little backpack and a bag full of snacks. The trip takes six hours. That's a long time. In fifteen minutes we get on our first train — the first of five.

I'm happy. Really happy.

The big train station clock ticks, and after sixty seconds the big hand wobbles and moves slowly — unbelievably slowly — one more notch.

At ten after, Laura and Phillip arrive. They're arguing.

"Where have you been?" I ask.

Phillip starts in. "Once again her ladyship here could not walk past the gumball machine."

Laura shrugs. "We have loads of time!" She looks at me. "Here, hold out your hand." And she presses a big handful of gumballs into it.

"Did you get the tickets?" I ask Phillip. He holds them up.

"Got them yesterday."

"You're such a freak," Laura says.

Then the train arrives and we're finally leaving.

The sun comes out. I have a seat next to the window and I close my eyes.

"I'll bet Mi was a cat in another life," says Laura. When I open my eyes she's wearing red sunglasses. "In the next life I want to be a cat, too."

Phillip makes a face.

"You see, Mi," she says, "people are divided into two groups. Those who like cats and those who like dogs. Just like with tea and coffee, showers and baths."

"Sweet or salty," Phillip adds.

"Exactly," Laura says. "And I think that cats have a better life. For one thing they're pretty. And they have soft fur coats. And besides that they just sleep. And people pat them and otherwise leave them alone. They can spend all their time doing whatever they want."

Phillip gives her a sarcastic look but says nothing.

"Unlike dogs," Laura continues, "they don't have to save lives, fetch sticks or lead blind people around. You see, Phil, cats simply have better lives."

Phillip grins contemptuously and looks out the window again. The landscape is still familiar. We have to change trains again in town.

"Mi was definitely a cat," Laura says again. "Look at her, Phil. The way she just looked around. That was pure cat! Maybe she'll even purr if you scratch her under the chin!"

"No, she just hums," he says, and he blows a bubble.

"You also have a cat face, my little kitten," Laura whispers to me. Then she jumps on Phil and starts to tickle him.

* * *

"What is it about these gum machines?" I ask Laura when we're standing on the platform at the train station in town.

"Not telling," she says.

"Gumballs aren't even that good," I say.

"I know." She looks at the schedule.

"I'll tell her!" Phillip says suddenly.

"You so won't!" Laura snaps at him.

Phillip pretends to be about to explain, until Laura finally says, "I'll explain it to you another time." Then she glares at Phillip and adds, "*I* will tell her!"

* * *

Lunchtime. Fanta, sandwiches. A tunnel and forests.

"Wha...what's your uncle like?" asks Laura with her mouth full.

"He's a music critic. I told you about him. He is very cool. Didn't make a big deal about us coming. Just wanted to know how many of us there were and what we wanted to eat."

"Great," says Laura. She takes a swig of Fanta and it drips down her chin and spills on her sweater.

I think about Dennis, Mum and Dad back at home,

about Suse and Ines at school. It all suddenly seems so far away and none of it matters when I think about it because the sight of Laura pushes all these thoughts away. The sight of her face with her damp lips as she smiles at me and then turns and looks out the window again. The sight of her is so sweet, and it hurts and feels good at the same time. I would like to never have to think about anything else ever again.

"So, my dears, now I'm going to sleep for a bit," Laura says, pulling her jacket up under her chin and leaning against the window.

Whoever came up with this face? This long straight nose with freckles and the green eyes, the straight black eyelashes, the mouth that looks as though someone painted it. So beautiful. She is beautiful, the way she sleeps. And when I tell her something and she listens to me. And when she listens to a new song, and when she's happy. Or sad. Always so beautiful.

I look over at Phillip and he smiles at me and then looks out the window.

Three more hours.

Here comes another tunnel.

13

When we arrive at the train station Phillip pulls a piece of paper out of his pocket.

"So, we have to find the streetcar — number 81. That will take us to Waldschlösschen."

He looks around. Laura looks around. The sun is still shining, it's cold and this is the first time I've been in this city. It is old and gray and dusty. It's beautiful here. The houses are old and the apartments in them probably have incredibly high ceilings. In our town houses like this would immediately be renovated and painted some weird color so that they wouldn't be gray any more. So that the people who live in the new-old expensive apartments can be happy that they don't live in an old gray house, but in one that's yellow. Or sky blue.

I'd rather live in a gray house.

"Let's go," says Phillip, and Laura pulls me by the sleeve.

The streetcar rattles. At the sixth stop we get out. The houses here are gray, too. There are pigeons and old fountains. People walking in the street.

We turn into a laneway up a gentle hill. We stop in front of a big house. Phillip runs his finger along the name plates.

"We're here!" Laura whispers in my ear.

The door buzzes open.

The stairs are dark. The only light comes through big green windows that seem to look out onto a courtyard. We climb three flights up. A door opens and in the doorway stands a man with reading glasses and spiky gray hair. He's dressed entirely in black. He shakes hands with Laura and me while Phillip introduces us.

"I'm Frank," he says. Then he gives Phillip a hug.

Laura grins at me.

"Come on in. Make yourselves at home. If you're thirsty, help yourself. If you're hungry, the same. Everything is in the refrigerator," he says, giving us a tour. He shows us the kitchen, the bathroom and two rooms — one with a big bed and another with a sofa. "I don't know how you want to arrange things. Two of you can have the guest room and one can take the study. Doesn't matter to me." Then he looks at his watch. "Unfortunately, as I told Phillip, I won't be able to join you this evening, but here's a key." He takes a ring of keys from a chest of drawers. "And here is my cell number in case you need anything. Otherwise I'll see you tomorrow morning."

And then he sweeps by us and out the door.

For a moment we just stand there looking at the door. Phillip is the first to move. He goes into the kitchen and

I hear him open the fridge. Laura hears it too and plunges after him.

* * *

"So, what's the plan?" asks Phillip, after he's put his dish in the dishwasher.

"Have fun," says Laura.

"Do you know your way around here?" I ask him.

"No. But we're right in the middle of town. Something must be going on. I think we should just leave it to chance. But first, ladies…" And he pulls Laura's tobacco pouch out of her pocket.

Smoking on a balcony again. I take a drag and look down at the street. The streetcar clangs around the corner and clatters up the hill. I take another drag. This time it isn't so bad.

Another streetcar. I imitate the sound it makes, and Laura and Phillip laugh.

And then we go out. We walk around the streets a bit and look in the shop windows. Junk shops. Fruit and vegetable shops. An old-fashioned cafe with lace table-cloths. And then we see a bar that looks cozy.

"Phillip, you get the drinks. You're the biggest," Laura says.

Phillip pushes through the crowd. Laura watches him, then suddenly she gives me a big hug and says, "It's nice that you came with us."

She holds me tightly. For an eternity.

Phillip comes back with three bottles of Beck's.

"They're pretty easy-going here. This is practically a student pub," he says. I look around. The bar is full, the music is loud.

So this is what university students look like.

My parents didn't stay in school. Dennis and I are the first ones in the family who might even be able to go to university. Dad had an absolute fit when Dennis once said that he didn't know whether he would bother graduating.

"Do you want to go to university?" I ask Laura. She shrugs her shoulders while she clinks her bottle against mine.

"Prost!" Then she raises her glass to Phillip. "What about you?" she asks me.

I look at the people in the bar and wonder what their lives are like. To wake up every day in your own apartment, in a city far away from a little town that you only talk about when someone asks you where home is. Always carrying books and papers under your arm, spending time in big libraries where you have to be quiet. Listening to professors, maybe even saying something yourself and maybe what I say might even be right.

"Yes, maybe," I say.

"And what do you want to study?" asks Phillip.

"I have no idea."

A couple in the corner have started to dance. Laura watches them and moves to the music. Then she leans over and asks me if I want to dance.

I don't. I'd rather watch the people. Laura stands up

anyway and goes over to the dance floor. Phillip drinks the last of his beer, raises his bottle and asks me if I want another. I rummage around for my wallet.

"Hey, don't worry about it. It's on me. You can pay for the next round."

Laura's eyes are closed. She's standing in the middle of the dance floor, and I wonder what song she is dancing to, what she is listening to in her head. All around her people are hopping around and flinging themselves against one another crazily, but no one touches her. She smiles.

Phillip comes back to the table with the beers and I try to finish up my first one in a hurry.

"Prost," he says, and we clink bottles. "Not many people drink as fast as I do."

"And that is just one of my many talents," I say. I try to peel the label off the bottle with my thumbnail. I have to think more about whether I want to go to university, whether I want to keep studying, and if so, what. Again I imagine myself climbing the stairs in a big old building, maybe hurrying to get to a lecture on time. The steps are old and made of marble. Big lecture halls filled with hundreds of students.

"What are you thinking about?" Phillip asks.

"Stuff."

"Aha." He nods and turns to look at the dance floor, too.

When they start to play a new song, he suddenly jumps up and rushes over to Laura, who has stopped dancing. He starts to dance — actually he just bobs around and moves his lips to the lyrics. Laura looks at him, her eyes wide, and grins. Then she comes over to me at the table again, takes a drink from her bottle. She takes her tobacco out of her jacket pocket and rolls a cigarette. She sticks it in her mouth, grabs the candle from the middle of the table and lights her cigarette.

"You know, in Hamburg you can get thrown out of a bar for doing this, because it means a sailor will die." I didn't know that. She inhales and blows out the smoke. The candle flickers. "Poor sailor."

Laura looks over at Phillip and smiles.

"That's the only song he'll dance to, the absolutely only one." Then she looks at me again. "Are you still going to dance with me today?" She shifts closer to me and leans her head on my shoulder, and suddenly I am back on the hill that night — her head on my shoulder. "Oh, please, Mi. Dance with me, okay?"

It's fun to dance with someone when you are only dancing for that person. To shout out the lyrics together if you know them, to be together inside a song. From now on every time I hear this song, I will think, that's the time I danced with Laura. That's the place where she put her arm around my shoulder. And on that night everything was right, because the DJ played the right song — maybe Madonna, Pixies or "Blister in the Sun" by the Violent Femmes — and because we were far away, in a completely different city. That was the time we simply took off for a trip to the east, and Ines and Suse stayed home. Because Laura just wanted to be with me.

We drink a lot. I pay for the next round. Then Phillip buys the next one because he's thirsty and doesn't want to wait for Laura.

I'm not drunk, just a little tipsy maybe. And I'm thirsty because I've been dancing so much.

Laura takes me in her arms and says, "You have no idea how much I love you."

How much do you, then?

Then the DJ puts on a new song and Laura sings along with the lyrics again.

* * *

Phillip is tired. There are only a few people left in the bar. Only one woman is standing alone on the dance floor and swaying to the music — not Laura this time, but I can't stop watching her standing there, hardly moving.

"Let's go," says Phillip. So we get our jackets. It's cold outside. Laura is still singing, "Into the sea, you and me," and she starts hopping around in circles on one leg. Phillip has sleepy eyes, and he doesn't say much.

At a fountain in the middle of a square Laura stops singing and pulls me by my sleeve onto the side of the fountain.

"So. We've waited long enough." She has to struggle a bit to keep her balance.

I stand there, wondering what she wants. Phillip just looks at her, too, until finally she says, "I want to hear you recite 'Erlking.' Please. Just for me. And Phillip." She looks around and adds, "There's no one else around to hear you."

Phillip laughs quietly, but the noise echoes off the walls of the houses and sounds louder than he intends.

"Please," says Laura as quietly as she can.

"Oh, yes, please," Phillip adds. "It's about time."

I think about it, and the first line comes to me. We had to learn "Erlking" by heart in the seventh grade. I got an A, and I still know it.

So, here in the middle of the night, in a strange city, I tell them the story about the father whose child dies while they're riding home.

> *The father now gallops with terror half wild,*
> *He clasps in his arms the poor suffering child;*
> *He reaches the courtyard with toil and with dread—*
> *But the child in his arms lies motionless, dead.*

Then I bow and Laura applauds, her gloves muffling the sound of her clapping.

And I jump down from the fountain and am not the least bit embarrassed.

14

Déjà vu. Once again we are lying together in a bed. On the way home we danced. Then we watched a horror film. Frank wasn't home and he still hasn't come back.

"I'll sleep on the couch," Phillip said, and we all brushed our teeth together.

We've really had fun.

"Are you asleep already?" whispers Laura.

I turn over.

"No."

"Good." And then she giggles.

Suddenly I am very nervous, because she doesn't say anything else. And it's dark. I can smell her and hear her breathing. My stomach feels very warm.

She just wants to be my friend. She doesn't want to kiss me any more.

"Are you still awake?" she asks again.

I nod. Suddenly she is very close to me.

"Really?" she asks.

"Yes."

"Awake?" she asks, and her mouth is very close to mine.

And then she kisses me very softly.

"A goodnight kiss so that you can finally go to sleep," she says.

She stays so close, though. What's happening?

The apartment door opens and closes.

"Shhh!" she says. We hear Frank pull off his shoes and put something on the floor. Steps. The toilet flushes. More steps. A door is pulled closed.

We keep listening.

"I am still awake," I say quietly. And then she kisses me. And again. Just little kisses. But soon more. And more. And longer ones.

I am getting warm. Laura slides closer to me and I move closer to her. Suddenly we are lying without the covers on. And we are kissing. Laura strokes me — first just my arm, then her hand reaches down and slowly moves up my leg. I hold her hair. It feels like feathers, so soft. I stroke her neck and we look at each other. There are no shutters, only curtains, and the streetlights are shining through, orange. Laura looks at me and slowly strokes my thigh. I'm wearing a T-shirt and panties.

Suddenly she stops, pulls her hand away and says, "I'm sorry, I…you…"

I sit up. And then I pull off my T-shirt and look at her. I take her hand and place it back on my leg.

Everything is very easy. To be naked is easy. Kissing, too. Her neck, her stomach. She kisses me back — my neck, my breasts, my stomach, and then she looks up briefly and smiles at me, and I close my eyes.

* * *

The streetcars are clanging again. I hear a door open and the drone of a radio. A coffee machine.

We lie here. We are both awake. I smile, because she is smiling.

"Breakfast," she whispers. I nod.

"What now, Laura?"

"I don't know," she says. "What now, Mi?"

I don't know. I get dressed. Underwear, T-shirt, jeans, sweater, socks. Laura does the same. Then we go into the kitchen.

15

We've been lying in bed a long time. It's eleven o'clock when we start breakfast and it gets later because Frank starts talking. But I can't listen. I look at Laura, at the clock, and I think, after another six-hour trip we'll be home. What then? Only six hours.

Phillip is checking to see which connections we take. I call home and leave a message on the answering machine asking Mum to pick me up at the station at nine o'clock.

Soon we leave. Every now and then Laura looks at me, then back down at the floor.

It is Sunday.

I hate Sundays.

* * *

"Why are you both so quiet?" Phillip asks when we're on the train.

"Don't worry about it, Phil," Laura says.

"I'm going to the bathroom," I say. When I close the

washroom door behind me, I lean against the wall and look at the shaky reflection of my face in the shaky mirror.

Do I look different? I think about last night and my stomach lurches. But then I think about home, and I feel sick.

When I go back to my seat, Phillip gives me a strange look. Then he stares deliberately out the window, a big frown on his forehead.

Suddenly he jerks his head back to Laura.

"And what happens to the two of you now?" he asks her. "You told him?"

Laura shrugs. "He guessed. He already knew." She searches through her bag and pulls out her pack of tobacco.

"No smoking in here," Phillip reminds her.

"Shit," she murmurs. She puts it back.

"Are you making it official? At school and stuff?" asks Phillip.

"Are you crazy?" Laura says.

"Why not? It's not a crime," Phillip says.

"No, it isn't a crime," I say softly.

"Anyway, it's nobody else's business," Laura says.

Then we say nothing more, just stare out the window.

* * *

The closer we get to home, the more restless Laura becomes. At one point she grabs her tobacco and says, "I'm going to find the smoking section." And then she leaves.

Phillip groans as she closes the compartment door behind her. Looks at me.

"What?" I snap.

"Nothing. Really." He sighs briefly and shakes his head.

"For God's sake, what's the matter?"

"Do you love her?" he asks finally.

"Yes! Why?"

"Because that's the most important thing, isn't it?" he says quietly.

I nod.

Laura comes back stinking of smoke.

"You don't even have to smoke yourself in the smoking section, it's that smoky in there. Can you believe it?" she says, and then she goes quiet again.

* * *

The stop after the next one is ours. I gather my things together slowly. Phillip also starts to get restless. Only Laura stays sitting in her seat, staring out the window. It got dark long ago.

When the train arrives, she says, "Home, sweet home." She stands up and gets her things. We get off.

Mum is standing in front of the station and she waves at me.

"Hurry up, I'm in a No Stopping zone." Then we drive off. Laura stands there and waves at me slowly as we drive past.

"So, did you have a good time?" Mum asks.

"Yes." Everything is different now.

"Did you behave yourself at this uncle's place? And thank him?"

"Yes." Maybe. Oh, shit, I have no idea.

"Leave your laundry out tonight and I'll throw it in the wash first thing in the morning."

When I was little, everything was simple and straightforward, and there was a solution to every problem. Now I suddenly don't know anything any more, and things just get more and more confusing.

Mum turns to me.

"Why couldn't you walk home from the station? Do you have any idea what gas costs?"

Maybe I was sleeping and I woke up, but I'm still dreaming.

That must be it.

16

Maybe this is a love story now. An affair. No. Not an affair. It's a secret. Laura and I see each other every day at school but that's all. Her mother has come home.

"I'll come over to your place later," she says. And then she doesn't come.

Nobody must know. Whatever it is is just for the two of us.

"You and me," she says as she kisses the end of my nose before Suse and Ines arrive. At home I wait for her. I listen to Annie Lennox on the tape that I have listened to hundreds of times — "I Love to Listen to Beethoven." Madonna. The Breeders and Edie Brickell. "This Is Not a Love Song."

But then, everything sounds like a love song. Absolutely everything.

It's weird at school. The days rush by, but nothing is important. Not the work that we copy down. Not Suse's new haircut, that she has to point out to me after the week-end. I just live for the small moments when we're alone.

This is nobody else's business. And Laura winks at me.

It's like when you make a wish. If you say it out loud, it won't come true. So I stay quiet and don't say anything.

It is what it is.

And Laura just says, "You and me."

And that's all that matters. She doesn't say anything else. No. It's not a crime.

* * *

"How come you didn't come yesterday?" I ask her on Thursday.

"I'm sorry." She gives me a little kiss, nothing more. "I'll make it up to you tomorrow evening. We can meet at my place, okay?" She smiles, takes my hand, strokes it lightly. Then we hear Suse and Ines coming and she drops my hand. The door opens and she sticks a cigarette in her mouth.

"We get our math assignments back today," says Ines, and Suse groans.

God, who gives a shit? I won't be alone with Laura until tomorrow. Not today. And she didn't say why she didn't come yesterday, either. Who cares about math?

They have no idea how little I care about it.

"So, Miriam, Ines says you've got a big crush on someone," Suse says. I can see on her face that she can't wait to hear all the details.

I look over at Ines, who is suddenly busy rummaging around in her backpack.

"What's his name?" She doesn't even seem to blink.

Laura hands me a cigarette.

"It doesn't matter," I say.

"What do you mean, it doesn't matter? You finally have a chance to lose your virginity and it doesn't matter?" Suse smiles.

If I were to tell her now…

"Maybe," I say, "I just have no desire to discuss my love life with someone who insists on telling us every fucking detail about her own shitty little life, whether we're interested or not!"

Ines holds her breath. Laura takes a drag on her cigarette and stares at Suse, too. Suse's smile turns wooden, and something in her glance seems to shift.

"Oh, so sorry that I'm always full of shit. So have you told Laura?"

"What is that supposed to mean?"

"Well, what do I know? The two of you are such damn good friends all of a sudden, eh, Laura?" She glances away from me. Out of the corner of my eye I can see the way Laura just shakes her head quietly and whispers something so soft that only I can hear it: "Suse, you pathetic little bitch."

Then everything is quiet. Nobody says anything else. Laura stands up when the bell goes and pulls me up. As I stand up I look back at Ines for a second, and then we leave.

* * *

FUCK IT ALL!

I am going crazy. I thought being in love was supposed

to feel good and right. None of this maybe-tomorrow-but-not-today business.

It shouldn't matter who you're in love with.

Now I'm at home. I am going to bake a cake, because I have to do something.

Flour, sugar, eggs, ground nuts, butter, vanilla, baking powder, a pinch of salt. That's it. Preheat the oven and spread the batter in the pan. Shove it in the oven. Sit on the floor and stare at the oven window for about an hour until the batter rises and turns golden.

I open the oven door and stick a toothpick in the cake. When I pull it out there's still wet batter on it. Needs a bit longer.

I wait. The kitchen smells good. I put on the kettle to make tea.

The water boils, I pour the tea and check the cake again. Now it's done. I take it out of the oven and smell it. Mum comes into the kitchen.

"How's it going, sweetie?"

"Good."

"Everything okay?"

"Yes." I drop the tea bag into the sink.

"Did you get your math back?"

"Yes. Got a B minus."

"Good." She stares at the cake. "Are you bored or something?"

"No. Yes." I take a cup out of the cupboard and pour myself some tea. It's too hot. I turn the cake pan upside down, but the cake doesn't come out.

"Mr. Lorenz couldn't stop talking about his son in biology class today," I say. "About how fantastic he is and all the stuff he's accomplished. And about how it would be good if we followed his example."

"Teachers' children!" Mum mutters.

I take a knife and carefully loosen the cake from the sides of the pan.

"And then someone asked him what he would do if he found out his son was gay."

"Who came up with that?"

"I have no idea. At any rate, Lorenz got really uptight and just said, 'My son is not gay,' and then the arguing went on until finally he said that if his son did turn gay, then he would no longer be his son." I've loosened one side of the cake so far.

"Men! Ask your father what he would do if Dennis suddenly came home with a boyfriend."

"Dad would make mincemeat out of him. But it's dumb, right? I mean, Mum, what would you do if I was in love with…another girl? Instead of with a guy?" One more side of the cake to go.

"Oh, honey, I don't think…" She hesitates briefly. "Well, as long as it was what you wanted, I wouldn't care if your friend was male or female."

I turn the cake over and it slides out of the pan. Then I turn and look at Mum. She's smiling. And behind her, standing in the doorway, is Dennis, and he is staring right at me.

17

I keep thinking about that night. And then I hear Massive Attack. *When there's trust, there'll be treats; when we fuck we'll hear beats.*

Funk. Weird.

When I stroke my belly and push up my shirt and feel the landscape of my skin, and when I feel myself, I hear myself breathing. When I pull off my shirt and my hand reaches down into my underpants and I feel warmer and warmer in my belly I get this feeling like, What's going to happen now, and I feel the hair between my legs and start moving to the rhythm of the music. Laura, I think then, as I breathe in and out. And all I want is her hand on me and to kiss her and not wait any longer.

Fucking isn't the same as making love. It's not about pink hearts and daisies.

And then I want to be loud, but I have to be quiet because Mum and Dad are light sleepers and the music won't drown out my sounds. That's when I want her here and it makes me crazy that she is on the other side of town, because she doesn't belong there.

When we fuck we hear beats. Here, right here. This is how it's going to be.

* * *

Today. Today is Friday.

I'm supposed to be at her place at eight. But at seven she arrives at my house with that look on her face.

"What's the matter?" I ask.

"Nothing." She goes out to the balcony, and I put on my pants, first one leg, then the other, and I pull them up and do them up.

She's lit a cigarette and she looks out over the neighbor's roof where a skylight is shining. It's Rudi next door, building his model airplanes upstairs.

"Tell me." I sit down beside her.

"I SAID IT'S NOTHING!"

I sit there and try to pull my legs up, but the bench is too narrow.

"I told Phil I was coming over. He'll be here soon."

That's just great.

I go down to the basement and grab a couple of bottles and take them back up to my room. My father never notices how many beers there are.

"Mi, I…" Laura starts.

I stand there with the bottles in my hand and wait, but she doesn't say anything more.

Then she takes me in her arms and holds me tight.

We don't talk much. Why do you need to talk when you can just look at each other, or hold each other's hands and feel each finger, feel how warm this other person's skin is, how it reacts to your touch. And when the music fits, the way it does now. Every song fits. Every song says, "Laura is here." Every song says, "Laura has landed, landed on my little planet, and she's here to stay and kissing me and smoking on my balcony." Every song tells you how good these moments are.

When Phillip comes, everything gets weird. We haven't said what we want to do so we just stay at my place, lighting candles and sitting on the balcony. The three of us, even though I imagined this evening would be different. We just sit here listening to music — Laura and I holding hands, Phillip wearing a sweater he's borrowed from me.

It's all so weird. It feels like the last night at summer camp, but I don't know why. Everything is very peaceful. Everything feels right, here on the balcony. Everything feels right.

Laura stays after Phillip leaves. She stays until late. She doesn't leave until after Mum and Dad are in bed. We say good night. A good-night kiss. And then another. Then more smiles and more kisses and more good-nights. Don't ask whether she's coming back or when we'll see each other again, just say sleep tight, just look up at the sky again and hold her hand a bit tighter.

Good night, Laura, good night.

Good night, Mi.

* * *

When I close the door, Dennis is standing there.

The hall is dark. Only the outside light shines through the glass of the front door. We stand there in silence.

Then he says, "Want to go back up to the balcony?"

I nod.

Dennis and I sit beside each other on the bench and freeze.

He starts to smoke.

Then he says slowly, "It's okay. Mum's right. Even if it's none of my business, it's okay." He holds out his cigarette so that I can take a drag. "Are you all right?"

I nod.

"Then it's all okay," he says.

PART III
The Big Bang

1

Laura isn't at school. Not on Monday, not on Tuesday, not on Wednesday. Maybe she's sick, though nobody else seems to care. I call her, but I just get the answering machine. I go over to her place, but no one answers the door.

One, two days without any message. At one point I find myself standing in front of a gumball machine. What did she really want here? I look and look, but all I see are gumballs. Small, different-colored balls.

I don't hang out in the girls' washroom in the mornings any more. I get to school right on time if I can, sometimes a bit late. Suse avoids me. Suddenly she's talking to Ines a lot.

On Thursday Laura still isn't at school.

I'm standing beside my bike, unlocking it.

"Hey!" It's Ines.

"Hey," she says again.

I fumble with the lock for a long time.

"I'm sorry," she says.

The lock springs open. I look up.

Ines is standing there with her hands in her pockets.

"I shouldn't have told Suse. I thought it was something nice for you, and I was so happy for you. But I should have known."

"Known what?" I'm holding the bike lock in my hand, the key swinging from it.

"That Suse is the last person who would be happy for you. I never should have told her." Ines gives me a crooked grin. "I'm sorry."

I know she means it. That she's not just saying it.

"Do you want to walk together for a bit?" I ask her.

She nods and takes the bike lock from me.

It's warm enough now to wear your jacket open.

"Where's Laura? Is she sick?" Ines asks, as we leave the school behind.

I shrug.

"Are you still in love?"

"Yes."

"And? Have you kissed?"

I nod. Then I look at her, because there's something in her voice, something about her tone that I haven't heard before. But I must be mistaken.

"That's good," she says, as she swings my lock through the air.

* * *

Friday. Saturday. Sunday.

And then Phillip comes over.

"Laura's gone," he says.

"What do you mean, gone?"

"She's gone to live with her father, in Cologne."

"But why?"

"How do I know?" Phillip twirls the end of his cigarette along the edge of the ashtray.

"Did you know she was leaving?"

"Sweetie, I was as clueless as you."

"Don't call me sweetie."

He opens his mouth to say something, then stops. "Sorry." He takes a deep drag of his cigarette.

I remember how Laura would hold in the smoke, how she always made this clacking noise in her throat, and how she would look at me and smile.

He butts out his smoke.

"Come on, let's go. Get something to drink."

I look at him.

"Come on. I'm inviting you." He takes my arm and pulls me up.

"No, I can't," I say. "I still have to…" But I can't think of what I have to do.

2

A few days later I get a letter in the mail. A big red envelope with my name on it.

Dear Mi,

I'm sorry that I didn't tell you before. Okay. I'm back in Cologne. Maybe you already know that. I couldn't take it with my mother any more. Or with school. Only you and I were right. I wanted to tell you everything on Friday, but I couldn't. I just couldn't. Do you understand?

I am trying to make a go of things here, again. Without you. I miss you already. Maybe things will work out here. I'll be back, but only as far as town, to pick up the rest of my things from my mother. If you want to see me, then let's meet on the eighteenth in the Austerhaus. Eleven o'clock at the bar. I'll be there no matter what.

Okay?

Laura

The note is too short to be a goodbye. There are no explanations, not the ones I need.

Then I feel something else inside the envelope. I turn it upside down and shake it. A little necklace with red beads falls out.

* * *

I imagine meeting Laura in the Austerhaus. I imagine us dancing, kissing.

Stay. Don't go. Why are you going?

I miss Laura. I have never missed anyone like this before. Never this much. It hurts each time. Why does it always hurt when I think about Laura? Always, always, always.

Don't go. The Austerhaus is big and loud and dirty and crowded.

I look at the envelope one more time. No return address, no telephone number. Nothing. Tomorrow's the eighteenth.

* * *

I take the train into town. I have no idea how I'll get back home. Maybe I won't go home again. Maybe Laura will take me with her. Maybe we'll go some place completely different. Just the two of us.

I haven't told anyone where I'm going. Not even Phillip.

I look at the clock. It's almost eleven. I haven't seen her yet. I look at the door to the bar.

Eleven o'clock. I am nervous. I have to go to the bathroom, but I don't want to miss her.

Someone taps me on the shoulder.

"Hey."

"What are you doing here?" I ask. How did he know I would be here?

"The same thing you are." Then he looks at my neck. "Nice necklace."

I wonder why she told him to come here, too. I'm mad. I wonder how many people are waiting for her here, even though I know that's stupid.

"So, is she here?" he asks.

"Do you see her?"

"For God's sake, how long have you been waiting?" Phillip waves to the bar man. Orders a tequila. "Want one?" I nod.

It's a quarter after eleven.

"The lady seems to be a bit late," he says.

"Maybe," I murmur. What if she doesn't show up?

"So do you have her actual address or phone number or anything?" he asks.

I shake my head. He orders us two more tequilas. I bum a cigarette from him.

What if she doesn't show up?

"Did Laura ever tell you how we met?" he says suddenly.

"At a party, right?"

"Yes, a stupid party. And the stupidest thing was that I was the one who threw it."

"And?"

"The party was bloody awful. But I wanted to practice DJing, so I invited everyone I knew. Someone brought Laura along. Or maybe she just came on her own."

I can just picture it. Phillip looks at the glass in his hand.

"Anyway, everyone got unbelievably drunk and threw up all over the living room and I don't know what else. But Laura was the only one who danced. And who stayed. She stayed until the very end. She made coffee for us and helped me clean up and…stayed. I wanted to throw her out with the others. But she just stayed."

"Now she's gone," I say. And there it is again, this feeling of fucking missing her, and I don't know if I will ever see her again, or if maybe she just doesn't want to see me. It hurts like shit.

Phillip takes my hand.

"Hey, come on." He sticks a tequila in front of my nose and we clink glasses. "What should we drink to?"

"To… I don't know."

"You can think of something. Come on."

I shake my head. He looks at me, raises his glass and says, "To all that's left behind."

We knock back the tequilas and then he pulls me up onto the dance floor and we dance.

* * *

It's the last song again.

This is the one she danced to. This exact same song. I am standing by myself on the dance floor and listening to each line.

I still remember you, girl from Mars. I still love you, girl from Mars.

As soon as the song ends, the lights go on. Phillip is standing by the wall holding my jacket. He just looks at me. Then he comes over and presses my things into my arms, and we are swept out of the club. I am sweating and feel clammy. Phillip doesn't look much better.

We go outside and just stand there for a moment, looking up at the sky. People walk by us.

"Hey," Phillip says suddenly. "It's really warm out."

I notice it, too. My body is slowly cooling off, but I'm not getting cold. The wind is warm and dry on my face.

"It's definitely getting to be summer," says Phillip.

I look at him doubtfully.

"No, really," he says. Then he looks up at the sky, closes his eyes. "Summer is coming. Definitely."

THE END